Be honest with **[me]**. **[What]** happened to y**[ou and]** your gun?"

"I'll tell you what y**[ou need to know. No]** more."

"Come on, John. I know I'm a rookie, but we're supposed to be working together."

"It's your job to do what I tell you," he said. "And stop thinking like a cop. That's not who you are anymore."

Her sharp gasp told him that his comment struck home. "You don't think I can handle this."

"I didn't say that."

"You didn't have to. I'm smart enough to read between the lines." Her voice rose. "I can be subtle."

"Go ahead. Announce it to the world."

She turned on her heel. "I'm getting out of here before I say something I will really regret."

He watched the angry twitch of her hips as she stalked back into the room and headed toward the door. "Lily, wait. Where are you going?"

"Don't worry. I can take care of myself."

And with that, she slammed the door behind her, effectively shutting him out.

Surviving this mission was going to be more challenging than he'd expected.

CASSIE MILES

NAVAJO ECHOES

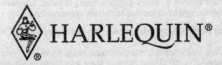

HARLEQUIN®

TORONTO • NEW YORK • LONDON
AMSTERDAM • PARIS • SYDNEY • HAMBURG
STOCKHOLM • ATHENS • TOKYO • MILAN • MADRID
PRAGUE • WARSAW • BUDAPEST • AUCKLAND

Cheers to the fantastic city of Denver, my home.
And, as always, to Rick.

Special thanks and acknowledgment are given to
Cassie Miles for her contribution to the
BODYGUARDS UNLIMITED, DENVER, CO
miniseries.

ISBN-13: 978-0-373-69266-8
ISBN-10:   0-373-69266-8

NAVAJO ECHOES

www.eHarlequin.com

ABOUT THE AUTHOR

For Cassie Miles, the best part about writing a story set in Eagle County near the Vail ski area is the ready-made excuse to head into the mountains for research. Though the winter snows are great for skiing, her favorite season is fall, when the aspens turn gold.

The rest of the time, Cassie lives in Denver where she takes urban hikes around Cheesman Park, reads a ton and critiques often. Her current plans include a Vespa and a road trip, despite eye-rolling objections from her adult children.

Books by Cassie Miles

HARLEQUIN INTRIGUE

820—ROCKY MOUNTAIN MYSTERY*
826—ROCKY MOUNTAIN MANHUNT*
832—ROCKY MOUNTAIN MANEUVERS*
874—WARRIOR SPIRIT
904—UNDERCOVER COLORADO†
910—MURDER ON THE MOUNTAIN†
948—FOOTPRINTS IN THE SNOW
978—PROTECTIVE CONFINEMENT††
984—COMPROMISED SECURITY††
999—NAVAJO ECHOES

*Colorado Crime Consultants
†Rocky Mountain Safe House
††Safe House: Mesa Verde

CAST OF CHARACTERS

John Pinto—This Navajo, veteran agent for Prescott Personal Securities prefers a logical, methodical approach...except when it comes to Lily, his partner on this case.

Lily Clark—The rookie agent and former policewoman is determined to make good on this assignment despite ethical challenges and a tendency to act first and think later.

Ramon St. George—The governor of Cuerva, a Caribbean island famous for offshore banking, financial trusts and its translucent blue sea.

Edgar MacAllister—A master of disguise, retired from MI6 but willing to help his old friend, Robert Prescott.

Robert Prescott—Founder of PPS, formerly with MI6, he's been in hiding for two years and is anxious to get back to Denver.

Evangeline Prescott—Robert's true love who runs the operations at PPS.

Kyle Prescott—Son of Robert and his first wife, Olivia.

Peter Turner—The wounded half brother of Kyle. Son of Olivia and her current husband, Stephen Turner.

Olivia Turner—Former wife of Robert, currently married to the head of Tri Corp. Media.

Clive Fuentes—Robert's former mentor, whose shady business dealings and offshore banking threaten everyone associated with PPS.

Chapter One

Their single-engine Cessna had been sabotaged. Both fuel tanks were empty. They were going down.

Through the cockpit window, John Pinto stared down at the turquoise expanse of the Caribbean Sea. His Navajo forefathers would be amazed to find their son facing death in this place so far from home.

The Cessna bucked and the water came closer, welcoming them into a cold, lethal embrace. He never should have deviated from the original plan....

LESS THAN AN HOUR AGO, JOHN HAD passed through customs in the Kingston, Jamaica, airport. Pulling their several suitcases on a dolly, he'd followed Lily Clark, his coworker at Prescott Personal Securities, through the glass doors to the curb.

Though John had never visited the Caribbean before, he'd been in subtropical climates and was prepared for the humidity. Some people called it sultry. To him, the moist air felt like a wet washcloth being slapped against his face. His research into the area told him that that median temperatures in July were in the mid-eighties.

He checked his wristwatch, already readjusted to the new time zone. Five twenty-seven in the afternoon. Not bad timing. They'd left Denver at dawn and made all their connections.

Lily spread her arms wide as if she intended to fly without a plane, soaring off into these milky blue skies on an errant breeze. "Glorious," she said. "Absolutely glorious."

Yes, she was. Lily was a tiny, blond package of pure energy. Only five feet, two inches tall, she looked like a pixie with her short hair and wide, whiskey-brown eyes. He'd been attracted to her since the first day she started work at Prescott Personal Securities, the premier bodyguard agency in the Rocky Mountain West. John found it hard to believe that Lily had once been a Denver cop.

She twirled once on her toes. Her sleeveless, tangerine-colored T-shirt outlined high breasts. Her knee-length khaki shorts revealed the tanned, well-shaped legs of an athlete. "Can you smell it?" she asked.

He sniffed. The airport stank of exhaust fumes from cars and taxis that hadn't been properly serviced. "What am I supposed to be smelling?"

"The sea. The fabulous Caribbean Sea."

Yeah, sure. Smell the orchids. Listen to the breezes though the silver thatch palms. Taste the rum. He wasn't in the mood. "We should check in with Inter-

Island Transport. Our flight for Cuerva leaves in fifty-two minutes."

"Is there enough time to grab a cab, race to the beach and stick my feet in the water?"

"No."

She bounced toward him. During this assignment, she was playing the undercover role of his girlfriend. They were supposed to be going to Cuerva for a romantic weekend. In her guise as his lover, she adjusted the collar on his black knit shirt and winked. Her fake flirtation was adorable and maddening at the same time. "Come on, John. Let's have some fun."

"I don't want to miss our flight."

She went up on tiptoe to whisper in his ear. "Nobody is going to believe you're my lover if you don't touch me."

Undercover identities weren't his favorite thing. Pretending to be someone else always felt like lying, which was probably why he and Lily had been paired for this assignment. John would handle the technical aspects. Lily would guard their identities and deflect suspicion.

She pointed to the dimple in her cheek with a shell-pink fingernail. "Give me a little peck right here."

"Fine." He wrapped an arm around her slender waist and leaned down, intending to kiss her cheek. Instead, his mouth found hers. A sizzling electricity shot through him, stirring passions he shouldn't be feeling for a coworker. The scent of her perfume tantalized him. How could she still smell like roses after a full day of travel? The taste of her soft lips surprised him. She was delicious. And this kiss was a big mistake.

She quickly pulled back. Her eyes narrowed as she whispered, "A little too enthusiastic, John."

He hadn't meant to kiss her. What the hell had he been thinking? "Sorry."

The corner of her mouth quirked up in a smile. "Are you really sorry?"

On a professional level, he regretted the kiss. But on a personal level? Being close to Lily was a constant temptation. She seemed to sparkle. Holding her in his arms was like catching a sunbeam.

"Hey, mon." A Rastafarian shuffled toward them in floppy sandals, moving to a musical beat that nobody else heard. Long dreadlocks flopped around his shoulders. A necklace of white shells contrasted with his ebony skin. "Are you John Pinto?"

"That's right."

"Well now, Mister John. I hear you and this pretty lady are looking for a ride to Cuerva."

"You heard wrong," John said. "We've already booked our flight."

The Rasta raised both hands and shrugged. His baggy Hawaiian shirt flapped around his narrow chest like the wings of an exotic bird. "I can give you the grand tour on my Cessna. She's named *Martina* after a fine lady with red hair like the sunset. *Martina* the Cessna. I can show you where the sea turtles go to mate."

"Wonderful," Lily said. "Let's go with him. It'll be much more interesting than a commercial flight."

Interesting? Taking off in a plane named after a redhead? With a pilot in dreadlocks who looked like he was having trouble standing up? Stiffly, John said, "Our arrangements are already made."

"My name is Edgar." The Rasta stuck out his hand. When John shook the long fingers, he felt a firmness and strength that caused him to take a second look. The Rasta's black eyes showed a seriousness that didn't fit with the costume. Quietly, Edgar said, "Miss Evangeline recommends my services, mon."

Evangeline Prescott was in charge at Prescott Personal Securities. She'd sent John and Lily on this trip to make contact with her husband, Robert, a former MI6 agent who was presumed dead and had been missing for two years.

Robert Prescott had founded PPS, and he was more than a boss. John had been one of the first agents hired, and he considered Robert to be his mentor and his friend.

"All right, Edgar," John said. "Do you mind if I make a phone call first?"

"Sure thing, mon."

They went back inside the air-conditioned terminal. While Lily chatted with Edgar, John opened the suitcase that held his computer and electronic equipment, including a satellite phone with a secure line. All communication with their office needed to be untraceable and indecipherable. Over the past several months, PPS had been investigating a series of murders back in Denver that might have roots on Cuerva.

With the three-hour time difference, he figured Evangeline would still be at the office. He got through on her private line. "Who's Edgar? And why does he want to show us where the sea turtles mate?"

"You can trust Edgar MacAllister. He's a friend." Evangeline's breathy tone betrayed her excitement at the prospect of being reunited with her husband. "Have you heard from Robert yet? Have you seen him?"

"We're still in Jamaica."

"Right. Of course, you are."

It was unlike Evangeline—a former FBI agent— to be so rattled. He asked, "Is there some reason why you kept Edgar a secret?"

"He contacted me this morning. The threat level on this assignment has gone from amber to bright red. Someone on Cuerva is after Robert."

"Who?"

"I don't have a name for you, John."

He'd expected complications. Otherwise, Robert Prescott could have hopped on a commercial flight and come directly to Denver.

"There's more bad news," she continued. "We've uncovered information that a Denver businessman with mob connections is involved in our murder investigations. His name is Drew Kirshner, and he arrived on Cuerva yesterday."

John put two and two together. Someone on Cuerva was after Robert. Drew Kirshner came here. "Is Kirshner the person who's after Robert?"

"I don't know." She exhaled a nervous sigh. "Be careful, John. Bring my husband back to me."

"Count on it," he said.

After he disconnected the call, he sat for a moment, assessing this new information. There were too many unknowns on this assignment, and the potential for lethal danger. It might be wise to pick up a couple of guns on Jamaica before heading to Cuerva.

As soon as he joined Edgar and Lily, he mentioned the need for additional weaponry.

"All taken care of, mon." Edgar pointed them toward the exit to the runways.

"Hold on," John said. "I need to cancel our other flight and see if I can get a refund."

The Inter-Island Transport representative was an intense brunette with a bun so tight that it lifted her eyebrows. She responded to John's request in icy tones. Their policy was to never issue refunds.

For a moment, he considered convincing her otherwise. John was an expert negotiator who learned to haggle when he was a skinny kid on the Navajo reservation selling crafts to tourists. But that was a long time ago, and he had more pressing concerns.

Lily popped up beside him. "What's wrong?"

"Wasting money goes against my grain."

"But this isn't really your money. The unused tickets can go on your company expense account."

"It's still a waste."

Her eyes were wide and curious, searching for answers. "Is there something you want to tell me?"

As if he would ever discuss what it was like to grow up dirt-poor, squeezing every nickel, going without dinner so his brothers and sisters could eat.

He'd never been a man who readily shared his life secrets. The less people knew about him, the better. Besides, he'd overcome his past. He was thirty-seven years old, respected in his field and financially successful. His family would never go hungry again. "We can talk later."

Her eyebrows pinched in a scowl. "That's the third time you've said that to me."

"And you still haven't taken the hint."

"Figuring you out is a challenge. And I'm very persistent."

"Like a migraine?"

"Like a thousand stinging wasps." Her innocent expression turned shrewd. "I already know a few things about you. You were in the Marines. You majored in physics in college, which led to your training and expertise in security systems."

"That's my résumé."

"I'll figure you out," she teased. "You didn't fool me at all when you pretended to be napping on the plane."

"I was sleeping. And so were you."

Edgar shuffled up beside them. "Let's go, mon."

Hoisting their luggage, he followed Lily and Edgar through the small terminal to the tarmac, where Edgar commandeered a modified golf cart and drove them to nearby hangars.

Apart from a painted picture of the glamorous red-haired Martina on the nose, the small, single-engine Cessna looked like a standard issue aircraft with a fixed undercarriage. Inside the cramped interior, John gave Lily the copilot seat and settled in behind them. As soon as they were airborne, he eased forward and took a position between the two cockpit seats.

The view was breathtaking. At the edge of sunset, the skies to the west had taken on a soft pink glow. From horizon to horizon, there was nothing but sparkling water as far as the eye could see. John soaked it all in. The beauty of Mother Earth never failed to amaze him.

He spoke loudly over the whir of the propeller. "Tell us about yourself, Edgar. How do you know Evangeline?"

Edgar's shoulders straightened. With quick, precise movements, he removed his earphones, then he unfastened a few clips and took off his hair.

Lily laughed out loud. "Great disguise."

"Thank you very much." Without the dreadlocks and the easygoing Rasta manner, he had the air of a gentleman. "I met Robert Prescott while we were both employed at MI6."

The British Secret Intelligence Service. Edgar had dropped the Bob Marley accent. He sounded British through and through.

"You're not with MI6 anymore?" John asked.

"Quite happily retired." His gaze fixed on the instrument panel. "I do, however, stay in touch with my former colleagues. When Robert requested my help, I was delighted to be of service."

"You've spoken to Robert," John said. "Is he well?"

"Very well, indeed. I'm not precisely certain about his plans, but I should inform you that this visit to Cuerva will be much more than a simple extrication."

John had feared as much. No one at PPS, not even Evangeline, knew what Robert had been investigating for the past two years, but it had to be huge. "You said the weapons were taken care of."

"In the rear empennage," Edgar said. "Remove the panel behind the fire extinguisher."

Hidden behind the panel was a beat-up Army-green backpack. Inside, John found two handguns and holsters. He immediately fastened on the ankle holster.

Returning to the cockpit, he handed the other weapon to Lily, who checked the clip and the balance before she tucked the gun and two extra clips into the carry-on bag at her feet. Her expertise in handling the Glock automatic reassured him. She might look like a pixie, but this lady knew how to behave in dangerous situations. He had heard that she was expert in several forms of martial arts.

"When do we meet with Robert?" she asked.

"Tonight at midnight," Edgar said. "In a place called Pirate Cove. You are instructed to wait for only one hour. If Robert does not appear, it means he's been detained and will contact you on the following evening at the same location."

Edgar leaned forward and tapped a dial on the control panel.

"Problem?" John asked.

"A malfunction with the fuel gauge. I filled up in Kingston, but the gauge shows we're almost empty." He pointed through the cockpit window at a speck in the midst of the vast turquoise sea. "Cuerva is dead ahead."

Dead ahead? That sounded ominous. John's gaze focused on the fuel gauge. The indicator edged closer to Empty.

"Rather a fascinating island," Edgar said. "A British protectorate, like the Caymans and Jamaica. The population is small, approximately eight thousand, and the residents claim to be descended from the infamous Caribbean pirates and escaped slaves from the sugar plantations in Jamaica. Cuerva was slow to develop its tourist trade."

"There are hotels now," John said. He and Lily were registered at the Grand Cuerva.

"The island's governor, Ramon St. George, has done much to encourage visitors. You'll probably meet him. He's a very visible presence on the island. Quite charming."

The engine coughed. John was beginning to think that the malfunction might be more serious than a gauge that needed adjusting.

"However," Edgar continued, "you should be advised that Governor St. George is a powerful and very dangerous man. His real interest lies in the establishment of offshore banking and financial institutions. He might be involved in money laundering or smuggling."

"Your plane isn't equipped to make a water landing," John said. He'd seen the wheels on the fixed undercarriage when they boarded.

"Ocean landings are notoriously choppy."

"I suggest you cut the speed to conserve fuel."

"I've already done so."

They were flying low. The island was close enough that John could see the outline of tall trees and a cliff above a white beach.

"Can you bring her down?" John said.

"I fully intend to try."

The engine sputtered and died. The propeller stopped. The reassuring whir was replaced with silence as the plane dipped lower. Out of fuel. They were going down.

THE CESSNA SHUDDERED SO violently that Lily couldn't tell if she was trembling or not. She was scared. That was for sure. They were going into a dive.

Beside her, Edgar pulled back on the yoke. His feet danced on the rudder pedals.

John yanked her out of the cockpit seat. "Back here," he said. "You'll be safer."

"We're going to crash."

"Yes." His dark eyes peered into hers as he fastened a seat belt across her lap. "Cover your head and hold on tight."

They plummeted lower. Her stomach lurched. There was nothing she could do but bend down and kiss her life goodbye.

The only mercy was that she didn't have much time to think about what was happening. Within seconds, they hit the water. Her world turned upside down. A tremendous impact. A fierce jolt that rattled her bones.

She was aware of the wind and the water as the

plane broke apart. Her shoulder crashed against something, and she recoiled. She felt a sharp pain in her head. Thrown free from the seat belt, she was falling.

The sea surged over her. Barely conscious, she tried to swim, but her arms and legs wouldn't respond properly. Had she been injured? Was she paralyzed? A wave splashed in her face, and she gulped salt water.

Her mind froze at the edge of consciousness, unable to process the most simple commands. She'd forgotten how to move, how to react, how to breathe. Helplessly, she felt herself sinking into the sea, and she knew this was the end of her life. She was going to die before she'd even had a chance to live. Only twenty-six years old. Still a virgin. Too damned young to die.

She felt herself being lifted, dragged back to the surface. John was holding her. "Lily, wake up."

Through a churning haze she saw him. His wet black hair plastered to his head like a seal. "Lily!" he shouted.

She blinked wildly. Her eyes stung. But she wasn't dead. The realization gave her strength. Her arms reached for him, clung to him. She gulped down air. Gasped. Coughed. "I'm okay."

Beneath the surface, his legs were moving, treading water and keeping them both afloat. Holding her with one arm, he pulled her toward a flat section of wing that floated like a raft on the water. "I want you to get up on this. Lie across it."

She struggled, fighting the numbness that threatened to overwhelm her. With John's help, she hauled her torso onto the wing and lay flat.

"Stay there," he said.

"What are you going to do?"

"Rescue our luggage."

His arms cut through the waves as he swam toward the tail of the plane that was gradually sinking beneath the waves. She saw Edgar helping him. They had all survived.

The two men swam toward her, dragging luggage that they threw onto the wing beside her. They aimed the section of wing toward the shore and began to kick.

"That was one hell of a belly flop," John said.

"Quite spectacular," Edgar agreed.

"We skipped across the water like a flat stone. Wish I had it on film."

"Indeed."

They were both laughing and grinning like idiots. She'd seen this reaction before when she was a police officer. Relief after intense danger affected different people in different ways. Some collapsed in shock. Some wept. Others screamed. Still others, like John and Edgar, made jokes and slapped each other on the back.

Edgar glanced over his shoulder. "I rather wish I could have saved the painting of Martina. She was quite a wonderful woman. I've lost her four times."

"How?" Lily asked. Her voice was a hoarse croak.

"Once in real life. Twice before in plane crashes. This will be the fourth."

Lily wasn't sure she'd heard correctly. "You've crashed three times?"

"Once on land in Costa Rica. That was bad. Almost lost my leg." He took a breath. "Once on water near the Florida Keys. Now this." Another breath. "I'm getting rather good at crash landing."

"Lucky for us," John said.

"Luck?" Edgar's voice struck a high, disbelieving note. "This crash had nothing to do with chance, dear boy."

"How so?"

"We were sabotaged," Edgar said. "We were meant to die."

Chapter Two

When they were close to shore, Lily slid off the section of wing into a rolling surf. She staggered toward the deserted beach that wasn't nearly as pretty as it had seemed from a distance. A thin strip of whitish-gray sand covered a jagged, rocky shoreline littered with bits of shell, rock and sharp coral from the nearby reefs. Untamed tropical forest reached almost to the edge of the water.

Not paradise, but she wasn't complaining. She was thankful to be on dry land, to still be alive. The crusty sand crunched beneath her feet as she staggered toward a thick log that had washed ashore, and she sat on it. Holding her head in her hands, she closed her eyes and exhaled a deep breath. Apart from an ache in her left shoulder and a ringing in her ears, she was physically okay. Her mental state was a whole different matter.

Behind her eyelids, she replayed the terror of sinking into the ocean, helpless to react, trapped in death's cold embrace. Never before had she felt so close to her own mortality. *Shake it off.*

She couldn't appear devastated. And definitely couldn't whine. Being chosen to accompany John to Cuerva represented a major upgrade in her work at PPS. She'd been given a chance to prove herself and didn't want to mess it up.

Opening her eyes, she saw him striding toward her with a bottled water in each hand. His black knit shirt outlined his muscular chest and broad shoulders. His wet khaki trousers clung to his thighs. He usually wore a suit in the office. This water-logged outfit was a whole lot better…sexier. Without even trying, John Pinto was hot. When he'd kissed her on the mouth at the Kingston airport? Wow! Her fingers reached up to touch her lips. Not even a plane crash could erase the memory of that kiss.

He squatted in front of her and held out the bottled water. "You're probably dehydrated."

"I almost drowned." But she knew what he meant, and the water tasted good going down. "Where did you get this?"

"I always have a couple bottles in my carry-on. Just in case."

"Always thinking ahead."

"Let's check you out." Holding her face in his large hands, he peered into her eyes. "Look to the right. Then the left."

She glanced both ways. "Like this?"

"Very good. Now look directly at me."

She focused on his deep-set dark brown eyes above high cheekbones and a strong, straight nose. God, he was handsome. Gratitude welled up inside her. This man—this incredibly brave, good-looking man—had saved her life. If he hadn't pulled her out of the water when she was sinking, Lily wouldn't have made it.

As she was about to thank him, his fingers probed the sore spot behind her temple and she reacted. "Ow. Am I bleeding? Will I need stitches?"

"The skin isn't broken, but you're going to have a hell of a lump."

His low baritone struck exactly the right note of gentle concern. He had a bedside manner that her parents—both doctors—would have applauded. "You know, John, I wanted to tell you how much I appreciate—"

"Have you ever had a concussion before?"

"I've knocked my head a couple of times but never completely lost consciousness. I must have a thick skull."

"Must have." He sat back on his heels and grinned. "You're tough for such a little thing."

A little thing? She swallowed the "thank you" that poised on the tip of her tongue. Her size had always been an issue for her. When she was a cop, half the guys in her precinct had called her Tinker-bell behind her back.

He touched the tender spot again, and she pushed his hands away. "Stop it."

"I know something about head injuries."

"If it's all the same to you, I'll wait for a real doctor."

She should have been kissing his feet and showering him with praise for rescuing her. Instead, she was irritated. Though he was great to look at, there was something about him that brought out the worst in her.

Masculine arrogance, she thought. In any given situation, he had to be the alpha dog, the leader of the pack. And she had never been a docile follower; she hated being told what to do.

However, if she was going to survive this assignment, she needed to start acting like a professional. Wrapping herself in poise, she said, "Thank you for saving my life."

"Anytime, rookie."

She glanced toward the tropical forest. "Shouldn't we be hearing an ambulance siren?"

"It's possible. Cuerva has a hospital and a few neighborhood clinics."

"How do you know that?"

"I studied up on the island. Memorized the topography and the major landmarks."

That was so like him. John was, by nature, a planner who prepared for every contingency. He'd probably made mental notes on what to do in case of a plane crash. "What's our current location?"

"We're on the far side of the island. Away from the hotels and the town. Cuerva is only about four miles wide, but there's a high bluff running down the center like a backbone. I doubt anybody saw our plane go down."

"So there probably won't be an ambulance?"

He frowned. "Do you need a doctor?"

The clanging inside her head had already subsided to a small tinkling bell. The worst part of the crash had been the panic, the shattering certainty that she was going to die. But here she was, alive and kicking. "I'll be all right."

"Then let's get moving." He stood up straight and glanced over his shoulder toward Edgar. "We should assess the damage."

Following him, she marched clumsily across the beach. The wet soles of her sandals slapped with each step. Even with the ankle straps, it was amazing that they'd stayed on her feet.

He pointed to two soggy pieces of luggage. "I could only save our carry-on bags."

Swell. Things just kept getting worse. "Most of my clothes were in the bigger bag."

"They're gone."

She was going to miss that yellow sundress she'd bought especially for this trip. And her favorite running shoes. "It's a good thing that you grabbed the carry-on. My wallet and passport are in there."

"And the Glock."

She remembered tucking the weapon into her bag before the crash. "Do you still have your gun?"

He tapped his ankle holster. "It got in the way when I was swimming, but I'm glad to be armed."

As soon as they got to the hotel, she needed to check and clean their weapons. A dip in salt water couldn't be good for the firing mechanism. "We can always buy new clothes. It doesn't seem like anything important was lost."

He shot her a dark, disbelieving glare. "We've

lost the computer, the satellite phone and all the other electronics I brought along."

Lily shrugged. She had little use for gadgetry. "I guess we'll have to rely on our natural instincts."

"Instinct won't provide a secure phone line for contacting Evangeline."

And, of course, the computer would have been handy for researching the island and doing background checks on potential suspects. "Maybe Edgar can help us out."

She looked toward the surf where Edgar stood watching as the tail section disappeared under the waves. All that was left of *Martina* the Cessna was the chunk of wing they used to get to shore.

He straightened his shoulders, made a sharp pivot and walked back toward them. "Rather an inauspicious start to your assignment. Have you reconsidered your plans?"

"For now," John said, "we'll proceed to the hotel and act as if nothing unusual happened. We won't report the plane crash."

"What?" she questioned. Not tell anybody? "That isn't even legal."

"I don't want to attract undue attention. We'll stick to the original plan, go to the hotel and check in."

"Very well," Edgar said as he gestured toward the forest. "Shall we locate transportation?"

"Wait a minute." Lily wasn't sure that she liked this plan. At the very least, John should have discussed it with her. "Somebody tried to kill us."

"And failed," John said.

"Well, it doesn't seem smart to pretend it didn't happen. Even if we don't report the sabotage, maybe we should go into hiding. Did you think of that?"

"I did," John said. "And I rejected the idea."

"Why?"

"Number one," he said as he held up a forefinger.

Lily groaned. "It's really annoying when you do the logic thing. The number one and two. Part A and Part B."

"Number one," he repeated, "this is a small island and we're obviously outsiders. We can't blend in."

"Speak for yourself. I'm good at disguises."

"Number two, if we're a visible presence, we might smoke out our attacker. Next time, we'll be ready for him."

That made a certain amount of sense. She and John were both well-trained and able to defend themselves. Still, she said, "If the bad guys think we're dead, we could use that to our advantage."

"Until we're discovered," he said. "Then what? We have no authority on this island. We can't arrest anybody."

"All right," she conceded. "We'll do it your way."

"Number three, we meet with Robert tonight. Then we can get this assignment planned down to the last detail."

Of course, that was what he really wanted. A detailed plan. Very rational. Very logical. She hated when John made sense.

BY THE TIME THEY REACHED THE Grand Cuerva Hotel, night had fallen. John tipped the bellman with a damp five-dollar bill and escorted Lily into the elevator, then headed to their prebooked suite on the top floor—the sixth. The Grand Cuerva wasn't the biggest hotel on the island nor the best. Obviously.

The "honeymoon" decor looked like Valentine's Day gone terribly wrong. The king-sized, canopy bed was draped in filmy red sheers that matched the curtains across the sliding doors to the balcony. Hearts loomed everywhere. A heart-shaped mirror over the dresser. Little heart vases. A red glass candy dish filled with—of course—hearts. There was even a red, heart-shaped Jacuzzi tub in the corner by the windows.

Lily stood in the center of the room, glaring. "There's only one bed."

"Honeymoon suite."

"We're not sleeping together. I want my own room."

Though the thought of seducing her had crossed his mind a few thousand times, he had no intention of acting on that desire. Still, he couldn't help teasing, "But we're supposed to be lovers."

"That was before somebody sabotaged our plane. The bad guys know who we are. There's no need to maintain undercover roles."

"Stop right there, rookie. It's dangerous to make assumptions without all the facts."

"The sabotaged plane is a fact."

"But we don't know the motivation. It's possible that we weren't the target. Somebody might have been after Edgar. I'll bet he's got a few enemies."

"Safe bet," she said. "But why would they choose

this moment to attack him? When we were in the plane?"

"Coincidence."

She scoffed. "I don't believe in coincidence."

With one hand fisted on her hip, her sharp little chin lifted, and her glare intensified. Clearly, she was moving into a confrontational posture.

And he didn't have patience to deal with an argument. In the crash, he'd been tossed around like a sock in a washing machine. His body ached, and his muscles were stiffening up.

Ignoring her, he strolled toward the Jacuzzi. Steaming jets of water seemed like good therapy.

"When I was a cop," she said, "I learned one important thing. The most obvious solution is usually the correct solution. Because we were in the plane, the sabotage was meant for us."

"You're not a cop anymore. The work we do is more subtle. There aren't as many hard-and-fast rules."

"I know. That's one of the reasons I wanted to work at PPS."

"Keep your mind open to the possibilities. All the possibilities. You're smart enough to figure things out, and I want to hear what you're thinking. But I have one hard-and-fast rule."

"What's that?"

"I'm in charge."

"Yes, sir."

Her tone was clipped, and he could tell that he was making her angry. Too bad. He was too worn out to be subtle with his explanations. "Here's what's going to happen. We make no assumptions until we talk to Robert and find out what his plan is. Tonight, we will parade around like a couple of dewy-eyed newlyweds. At midnight, we go to Pirate's Cove and meet Robert. Is that clear?"

Her full lips pinched together. A pink flush crept up her throat. "Perfectly clear."

John leaned across the Jacuzzi and turned on the faucets. The gush of water into the red, heart-shaped tub looked like a giant mouth gargling. "And now, I'm going to take a soak."

"Here?"

"Right here. Right now."

He pulled his knit shirt over his head, revealing the waterproof money belt fastened around his waist. She'd teased him when he'd first put it on, called him a nerd. But this handy belt had kept his passport, his company credit card and his money relatively dry. He peeled it off and glanced in her direction.

The pink in her cheeks had deepened to a bright scarlet. Through tight lips, she said, "You know, this might count as sexual harassment."

"Sue me." He tossed his shirt into a puddle on the floor. "I'm tired and sore. And the dried salt water on my skin itches like hell. If you don't want to watch, turn your head."

She darted forward and grabbed the money belt. "I need your credit card. I'm going downstairs to the lobby and, um, getting something."

He unfastened the top button on his trousers. "If it's food you're looking for, we can call room service."

"Clothes," she said. "I need something to wear. There was a shop downstairs."

"Good thinking, rookie."

As she fled from the room, he dropped his trousers, kicked them aside and stepped into the hot water. He positioned himself so the pulsating jets massaged his left hip, where a large bruise was already turning black and blue. The heat penetrated his body, easing the stiffness. Oh yeah, this was good. The only thing better would be if Lily agreed to give him a rubdown, which he assumed, from her rapid retreat, wasn't likely to happen.

His gaze flicked around the room, resting on one heart-shaped object to another. This sure as hell wasn't the way he'd pictured an idyllic island weekend with a lover.

AFTER SHOPPING AND DOING SOME serious damage on the company credit card, Lily returned to the ridiculous honeymoon suite to find that John had ordered room service. She took her own quick shower and changed before joining him at the table. Still irritated, she was giving him the silent treatment.

As the senior agent, he had the right to issue orders and decide the agenda, but his striptease went far outside the boundaries of acceptable behavior. And the worst part? *He wasn't even trying to turn her on.* All he wanted was a soak in the Jacuzzi.

To be honest, she was angrier at herself than at him. She was the one who'd gotten all hot and bothered. When he'd taken off his shirt, her pulse had raced to a hundred miles an hour. Though she'd tried to avert her gaze, she couldn't help staring at his bronzed skin and the defined muscles in his arms and chest. To see him naked? Oh, lord, she didn't think she could stand it. And yet, she'd felt the urge to stand and watch, to climb into the Jacuzzi with him, to rake her fingers through his thick, black hair.

Primly eating the room service burger and fries, she retreated behind her familiar boundaries of self-restraint. Not that Lily was a prude. Far from it. But sex hadn't been an issue during her college rebellion when she was mostly traveling and didn't want to be tied down with a relationship. Then, she'd been a cop and spent most of her time hanging around with other cops. Any hint of vulnerability would have made her life a living hell. It was safer not to get involved.

And now? Maybe it was time to lose her virginity, to wave the white flag of surrender and succumb. But not with John Pinto. He was her coworker—a senior agent who probably wasn't attracted to her the way she was to him.

Though she'd had enough time to calm down, she still couldn't look at him without drooling. Not even the garish flamingo-patterned Hawaiian shirt she'd bought for him in the hotel shop dampened his outrageous sex appeal.

She forced herself to concentrate on revenge. Oh, yes, she was going to get even. She didn't know how or when, but sometime—sooner or later—she'd get him all hot and bothered and then walk away. A dangerous game of sexual one-upsmanship. But he'd made the first move.

Apparently unconcerned by her silence, he took the last bite of his hamburger and checked his wristwatch, which was, miraculously, still ticking after the crash. "Nine-thirty," he said.

Which was two-and-a-half hours before they were scheduled to meet Robert at Pirate Cove. She chose her words carefully; John had already warned her that their room might be bugged. "How long will it take to get there?"

"It's about three miles from here. A forty-five-minute to an hour walk. Less if we jog."

She groaned. Though she regularly ran a five-mile workout in the morning, today had been strenuous. Surviving a plane crash wasn't part of her daily regimen.

She stood and stretched. "I need to keep moving around. If I sit too long, I'm going to stiffen up."

"I recommend the Jacuzzi."

"I'll bet you do."

She stepped through the sliding glass doors onto the balcony. The sound of calypso music rose from the beach where the hotel was sponsoring a party. A sea-scented breeze teased her senses. Though misty clouds drifted across the night sky, she could still see the shimmer of moonlight on the rolling waves.

John stepped up to the wrought-iron railing beside her. He had designated the balcony as a bug-free area where they could talk more freely. Still, he kept his voice low. "Have you checked the guns?"

"They'll work." The Glock automatic tucked into an ankle holster under her loose-fitting beige linen slacks was a reassuring weight. On top she wore a gauzy orange halter—a scrap of material that cost a fortune in the hotel shop.

"You look good," he said.

Despite her vows of revenge, she responded to his sexy baritone with a shiver of excitement. "Thank you."

"I hardly notice the bump on your head. You look almost normal."

"So glad that I'm not too freakishly grotesque."

Saying she looked "good" wasn't a compliment on her appearance; he was merely assessing her condition.

"We should join the beach party," he suggested. "Do some mingling. See if we can pick up any leads."

"Like finding out who wants to kill us?"

"Could be useful information."

Though she wasn't in a party mood, mingling sounded better than spending the next two-and-a-half hours alone with John, imagining what he'd look like in that cheesy red-curtained bed. "I'm ready if you are."

When they got off the elevator in the hotel lobby, her senses went on high alert. In her prior bodyguard assignments, she'd learned observation techniques, which meant keeping her gaze mobile and watching for anything out of the ordinary. She linked her arm with John's and turned her head toward the right. The hotel shop where she'd bought their clothing was closed, but the drugstore was still open. A bored-looking clerk rang up a sale and handed a pack of chewing gum to a husky tourist in baggy shorts and a Hawaiian-print shirt. He ran a hand through his short-cropped brown hair. The back of his thick neck was sunburned a dark red.

Even from the back, Lily noticed something familiar about that guy. His posture? The gesture of massaging his scalp? He reminded her of someone she knew in Denver, but she couldn't quite place him.

She heard a crash from the opposite direction and turned to see a waiter scrambling to pick up the scattered remnants from a room service tray. The reservation clerk at the front desk snapped angrily at the clumsy young man, and he responded with an insult about the clerk's mother.

When she looked back toward the shop, the husky tourist was gone.

TED HAWLEY PEEKED OUT FROM behind the rack of magazines in the hotel drugstore where he'd taken cover when Lily had glanced in his direction. He was pretty sure that she hadn't recognized him.

As she strolled out the door, arm-in-arm with that tall Navajo, she made some comment and laughed. If he hadn't known better, he would have believed that they were lovers on vacation instead of interfering agents of PPS.

It was his job to make sure they didn't hook up with Robert Prescott—his real target. Prescott needed to die here on Cuerva. The killing of Lily and

her boyfriend was a bonus. When he saw them with the Rasta pilot, he came up with a quick way to handle this assignment. Sabotage the plane. It was easy—too easy. They'd survived.

Cute, spunky little Lily Clark led a charmed life, always came out on top. Sure, she was a pretty little thing with her high breasts and her round ass. She'd even looked good in a cop uniform. Not many women could pull that off.

But he knew she wasn't so sweet and innocent. She'd humiliated him, made him a laughingstock at the precinct. He knew her for the gold-plated bitch she really was.

He was almost glad she'd gotten out of the plane crash alive. He wanted her death to be more personal. He smiled as he adjusted the collar on his black-and-yellow patterned shirt. There were so many slow, painful ways she could die.

Chapter Three

After his years as a bodyguard for celebrities, captains of industry and politicians, John was accustomed to finding himself in spectacular surroundings. Fancy-dress balls. The ski resorts in Aspen. Yachts the size of cruise ships. Custom-designed jets with full bedrooms.

He had trained himself to ignore the ambiance and concentrate on watching and listening for signs of trouble. With Lily at his side, he circled the lit swimming pool on the patio and descended a few stairs to the beach—a long stretch of white sand bordered by silver thatch palms, leafy shrubs and a profusion of exotic flowers that, even in the moonlight, were colorful.

Near the bar, dozens of tourists had gathered. Mostly couples, they danced to the lazy calypso beat. John should have been studying these people, some of whom might want him dead. He should have been looking for hidden weapons, furtive glances and other subtle signals of guilt. Instead, his gaze drifted toward the luminescent waves. The sea breeze kissed his skin, and the exhaustion he should have been experiencing faded away. The music of the steel drums and stringed instruments made him want to dance. He wanted to order a sweet rum drink with an umbrella from the bar in a tiki shack, to kick back and revel in this Caribbean night.

Beside him, Lily's wispy blond hair framed her upturned face. She'd been angry at him before, but now her smile seemed friendly. Or maybe she was a good actress playing her part as his lover.

"I know we shouldn't dance," she said.

She was right. One of the keys to keeping visual surveillance was to avoid participating in distracting activities. They should be standing to the side and observing the crowd. But sometimes a man had to go with his instincts. "One dance won't hurt."

When he grasped her small hand and pulled her toward the other couples who were barefoot on the sand, she frowned. "Are you sure about this?"

"When is the next time I'm going to be on a Caribbean island with a beautiful woman?"

She slipped off her sandals, and he did the same. The sand was soft beneath his feet. It had been a long time since he'd been dancing and that had been in a country-western bar with boot heels stomping on a hardwood floor. This exotic calypso music was different, more sensual. He allowed the drum beat to resonate inside him, stirring his blood.

Lily's movements were supple and graceful. A ripple started at her hips and rose through her torso and shoulders. Definitely sensual.

When the guitar player took over with a slow ballad, Lily drifted into John's arms. Her upturned face in the glow of moonlight and tiki torches was ethereal. The face of an angel.

"One more dance?" she asked.

"At least one more."

Her body molded against him. Despite the thirteen-inch difference in their heights, they fit together well. Her head rested below his shoulder. Her breasts rubbed against him. As they shuffled together in the sand, her thighs touched his, and he felt himself becoming aroused. Not the reaction he wanted, but he couldn't help it. She was too enticing, too delicious.

He tried to concentrate on other things, mentally dissecting the music into individual numeric tones, trying to remember the names of the surrounding flora. Orchid. Hibiscus. Periwinkle.

But Lily was pressing more tightly against him. No matter how much he wanted to control himself, it wasn't going to happen. He was erect and hard as stone.

Leaning back in his arms, she gave him a sly smile and lifted one eyebrow. She knew exactly what kind of effect her nearness was having on him. "Payback," she said.

"For what?"

"Your little striptease in the honeymoon suite."

But he hadn't been trying to seduce her. All he wanted was to wash off the sea scum. So what was her message? If anybody was going to be sexually intimidating, it was her? "I don't want to play this game."

"Do I win?" she asked.

"Hell, no."

"Game on."

When the ballad ended, they separated. Trying to regain his composure, John scanned the crowd. A group of new arrivals seemed out of place. They were dressed in silk business suits instead of casual beach clothes, and they didn't look like they'd come to party. The tallest was a heavyset black man with a goatee, clearly the leader. His gaze focused on John. When their eyes met, he didn't look away.

Beside him, Lily was alert to the potential threat. In a whisper, she asked, "Do you recognize him?"

John leaned down, pretending to kiss her ear. "He sure as hell seems to know me."

As they danced closer to the well-dressed group, John overheard an introduction. The tall, barrel-chested man was the appointed governor of Cuerva, Ramon St. George.

Edgar had warned them about the governor's possible involvement in smuggling and money-laundering through the offshore banks. He and his entourage of four—two who were obviously body-guards—seemed to be at this party to meet and greet, encouraging the tourist trade.

John approached the group. He introduced himself and Lily. "Cuerva is a beautiful island. We're going to tell all our friends to come here."

Ramon's lips spread wide in a voracious smile. "John Pinto is an unusual name. May I ask your heritage?"

"I'm Navajo. I grew up on the reservation in Arizona."

"An American Indian." His accent was part British and part local, and he sounded thrilled, as though John had told him that he'd arrived from Mars. "Well, John Pinto, you might be the first Navajo to visit our little island. Do you still live in Arizona?"

"Denver," John said.

"A grand coincidence," Ramon said.

Lily dug her elbow into John's ribs, reminding him that she didn't believe in coincidence.

The governor continued, "We have another visitor from Denver. His name is Drew Kirshner."

"Small world." One in which a governor of a Caribbean island was linked with a businessman connected to the Russian mob in Denver. Why would Kirshner be here? Several possibilities presented themselves. All were negative.

Lily kept the conversation going. "We'd really like to try some of the local foods. Do you recommend any restaurants?"

He waggled a forefinger at her. "I cannot choose just one. The others would be insulted. But I can warn you that many of our dishes are very spicy."

"I love hot food. And all these wonderful fruits. Mangos and guava."

She played the role of innocent tourist to the hilt, leading the governor and his entourage through a litany of small talk, even soliciting a recipe for curried goat that was used by the governor's housekeeper.

John wasn't sure where she was headed with this

chat until she slipped in a casual question. "I'd really like to know how to make that dish. May I stop by and talk with your housekeeper? If it's not too much of an imposition."

"I have a better idea," Ramon said. "Tomorrow afternoon at four, I am hosting a cocktail party at the governor's mansion, where many of our local specialties will be served as appetizers. I would be pleased to have you join us."

"Thank you, Governor," Lily said. "You're so gracious. We'll be there."

After a few more words, they rejoined the throng of dancers on the sand. John leaned close to her ear. "Nice work on wrangling that invite."

"Like Sun Tzu said—keep your friends close and your enemies closer."

"You think the governor is an enemy?"

"He's suspicious, especially since he knows Kirshner."

John agreed. When Lily put her mind to the task, she had the makings of a damned good agent. Not that he intended to tell her so. She had plenty of ego without his compliments.

AT ELEVEN O'CLOCK, THE NIGHT was still warm, but Lily was glad that she'd purchased a couple of black sweatshirts to cover their colorful island clothes. They needed to be subtle and careful as they headed out for their midnight meeting with Robert Prescott.

As soon as they left the hotel, John pointed out the small, dark man who followed them at a consistent twenty-foot distance, stopping when they stopped and starting up again when they moved on. They meandered along the main road in town, crossing from one side of the street to the other. Most of the storefront shops were closed, but the restaurants and taverns were still open for the tourists. She paused to look in a window and turned her gaze toward the street behind them. For a moment, she thought they'd shaken their silent pursuer. But no. "He's still there. Who sent him?"

"Your new best friend. The governor."

"Because I wanted the recipe for curried goat?"

"You know why we're being followed," John said.

Because they might lead the way to Robert Prescott. In spite of the easygoing Caribbean atmosphere, she was aware of the long grasp of danger that reached all the way from Denver to Cuerva. Other agents at PPS had been threatened. They had lost one of their own.

The reappearance and return of Robert Prescott signaled the end game. The final solution. And someone wanted to stop them.

John checked his wristwatch. "We're running out of time."

"How far to Pirate Cove?"

"Three miles. We can follow the road that runs along the perimeter of the island and then cut down to the beach."

"Why not start on the beach? We could swim."

"Bad idea."

She resented the way he dismissed her suggestion without even considering it. "Why?"

"On the beach, there's no cover. We'd be too obvious. And if somebody wanted to shoot us—"

"No way. If this guy intended to gun us down, he's had plenty of opportunities."

"Not really. I've kept to populated areas."

"It's a long walk." She shuffled along beside him. After the freedom of dancing on the sand, her sandals felt like bricks strapped to her feet and the idea of another cross-island trek almost brought tears to her eyes.

He pointed to a colorfully painted bench beside a beige stucco wall. "Wait here."

Splitting up seemed like a terrible plan, but she did as John ordered, sinking onto the bench, bending down to massage her calf and putting her ankle holster within easy reach.

John didn't go far. He approached a young man sitting on a beat-up motor scooter. After a quick negotiation and an exchange of cash from John's money belt, they had transportation.

"Did you rent this?" she asked.

"Bought it."

His extravagance surprised her. "What about the expense account?"

"I'll resell when we're done. Maybe even turn a profit."

She perched behind John on the scooter, which was only slightly larger than a moped and not much faster. Top speed was probably about thirty miles per hour, but it was better than walking.

On the scooter, they doubled back, passing the

man who had been following them. He jogged after them. John whipped onto a side street, then took a couple more zigzags. Then, they were on an unlit two-lane asphalt road, bordered by thick vegetation on either side.

Despite the crowds in town, there were no cars out here. She held on to John's waist for balance, but her gaze fastened on the road behind them. If the man who had been following them gave pursuit, her backside presented an obvious target. She saw no one. No headlights. No light at all except for the full moon. No sounds but the putt-putt of the scooter and the squawks of island parrots.

The entire island was only sixteen miles from end to end, and it didn't take long to get to the far end, where John turned right onto a road that was little more than a bike path. At a rocky strip of beach, he stopped. "This must be it. Pirate Cove."

"How are we doing for time?"

He checked his watch. "Six minutes to midnight."

While John hid the scooter in the lush undergrowth, she found a shadowed hiding place near the shore. She sat with her knees pulled up and her back leaning against the limestone.

She could see how Pirate Cove had gotten its name. Jagged rocks thrust into the sea, creating a natural barrier where smugglers could hide. Blackbeard and his crew of buccaneers might have rowed ashore to this very place and buried their treasure of gold doubloons.

John joined her and stretched his long legs out straight in front of him.

They sat quietly. Exhaustion rolled over her like waves from the sea, but her mind was still active. "I've been thinking about what you said earlier."

"About what?"

"You reminded me that I'm not a cop anymore."

"Right."

"That badge comes in handy," she said. "If I were a cop, I wouldn't have spent the past hour dodging through town, evading a tail. I'd arrest the creep and move on."

"Simple," he said.

And nothing about PPS was simple. "Our work is way more complicated than regular law enforcement. We don't have the authority to lock up the bad guys. On the other hand, we're not limited by a need for search warrants and chain-of-evidence procedure."

"For someone like you, someone who acts on instinct, that ought to make a positive difference."

She liked the freedom of thinking outside the box, but some of the things their job required bordered on being illegal. Like not reporting the plane crash. "It's a little confusing."

"How so?"

"Have you ever been asked to do something you thought was wrong? Like being a bodyguard for somebody who wasn't a good person."

"That's happened," he said. "But I didn't think it was morally wrong. Even scumbags deserve protection."

"How do you know you're doing the right thing?"

When he turned toward her, the moonlight cast an intriguing shadow below his high cheekbones. "I trust in what I'm doing because I trust the vision of Robert Prescott, who founded PPS. He's a good man. No matter what he asked me to do, I'd do it. Without questions."

She'd heard so many stories about Robert Prescott, the former agent for the British secret service who was involved in dozens of international conspiracies. After he supposedly was killed in a fiery plane crash in Europe, the legends got bigger. Robert Prescott came off sounding like a combination of a superhero and James Bond. "You've been with him a long time. What's he really like?"

"He has the qualities I respect. A sense of honor. Courage. Loyalty. He loves his wife, Evangeline, with all his heart."

And yet, he'd stayed away for two years. There must have been compelling reasons. Soon Lily would know. Soon she would meet the legend himself. Excitement stirred her senses. Here she was on a Caribbean island in a place called Pirate's Cove, waiting for a former MI6 agent. Life didn't get more exotic than this.

John checked his wristwatch. "He's late."

"Edgar said we should wait only an hour."

She hoped they hadn't come all this way to find a dead end. In spite of her sweatshirt, a shiver went through her.

"Cold?" John asked.

"A bit."

"Lean against me." He slung an arm around her shoulder and pulled her close. "I'll keep you warm."

"I'm fine." Right now she had the advantage in their game of sexual one-upsmanship, and she wanted to keep it that way. Shrugging off his arm, she repeated, "Just fine."

"I'm not coming on to you, Lily."

The hell he wasn't. "Of course not."

"Think of me as a big brother."

"Can't do it. I was an only child."

"That explains a lot."

He folded his arms across his chest and stared out to sea. As always, his attitude was calm, controlled and absolutely maddening.

She peered around his shoulder. "What does my being an only child have to do with anything?"

"No siblings," he said. "You never had to learn to compromise."

"Oh, please." She got along well with other people. "Spare me the cut-rate psychology. Both my parents were doctors, and I was sent to a shrink at the first sign of rebellion."

"And how did that work out?" he asked drily.

"What are you hinting at?"

"You're still a rebel."

"Maybe so," she admitted. Definitely so. The more people told her that she shouldn't do something, the more she wanted to give it a whirl. "I like to go my own way. What's the point in following the predictable path of college and career, marriage and kids?"

"Security."

He answered so quickly that she knew this was an issue he had considered. Doing what was expected. Being like everybody else. And yet that description didn't fit John at all. For one thing, he was thirty-seven and not settled down with wife and kids. "Have you ever been married?"

He gave a quick shake of his head. "You?"

"No." She hadn't even lost her virginity yet—a detail she didn't intend to share with him.

"How did you end up at PPS?" he asked.

"Long story."

He grinned. "You don't seem to mind telling long stories."

"I've got nothing to hide. What you see is what you get."

"We've got an hour to kill," he said. "Tell me all about yourself."

"I stepped off the predictable path when I dropped out of college in Ann Arbor."

She told him about backpacking through Europe, working as a waitress when she could and picking up the languages.

After seeing injustice on a global scale, she'd felt the need for order. That was when she'd moved to Denver and entered the police academy. "Then I joined PPS. It feels like this is where I belong. I love the people in the office. Former FBI agents like Evangeline and Melissa. Jack Sanders was an Army Ranger. Cameron Morgan, the cowboy." Her gaze bounced into his eyes. "Then, of course, there's you."

"What about me?" he asked suspiciously.

"You're very secretive. The strong, silent type. All I know about you is your work. You're an electronics genius and an expert in security systems."

"I like detail work."

No surprise there. He was a master of precision and planning. "Tell me about growing up. Did you have a big family? Were you good in school?"

John checked his wristwatch again. "We've waited an hour. Robert isn't coming tonight."

How typical of John to divert the subject as soon as it shifted to him. She followed him across the sand to the bushes where he'd hidden their transportation. Climbing onto the back of the motor scooter, she wrapped her arms around him and rested her cheek against John's broad back.

In a moment, they were back on the road, headed back to the hotel. She snuggled closer. Hanging on tightly wasn't really necessary; they were only going about twenty-five miles an hour. But she liked holding him. Her attraction to John was far from sisterly fondness. He was much too sexy to ever be thought of as a brother.

She heard him curse, sat up straighter and peeked around his shoulder. Headlights. A big vehicle. A Hummer. And he was coming right at them.

As the motor scooter skidded off the narrow road, she heard herself scream.

Chapter Four

The motorbike careened wildly. John clenched the brake. He fought for control.

The headlights swerved toward them. This wasn't an accident. The Hummer was coming right at them. The son of a bitch meant to run them over.

John swung hard right, finding a narrow pathway through the thick foliage. Low branches lashed his arms and shoulders. Lily's arms tightened around his midsection. The front tire ricocheted over rocks and exposed tree roots.

With nowhere else to go, he had to stop and stop fast. It was a damn good thing that this was only a scooter instead of a heavy motorcycle that would crush them both. Maneuvering so he wouldn't fall on top of Lily, he crashed sideways into a shrub, taking the impact on his thigh. He yanked her off the bike onto the ground beside him.

"Stay down," he ordered as he drew the Glock from his ankle holster, positioned himself on one knee and took aim.

His vision faded. Edges blurred. The wavering shadows from branches and fronds in the moonlight became dim, murky shapes. He blinked hard. *Not now, damn it.* This was the worst possible time for his eyesight to fail.

The fronds and branches became indistinct. All he could see were the bright lights of the Hummer. It would have to be enough. He fired three times in rapid succession.

Beside him, he heard Lily moving around, probably with her own weapon drawn. If anything happened to her, he'd never forgive himself. "Get down," he repeated.

"Like hell."

From the direction of the road, he heard the slam of a car door.

"Go home," came a yell. "Leave Cuerva now."

John pointed his gun toward the voice and fired again. Shooting blind.

He heard the vehicle pulling away and sank back onto the ground. Eyes closed, he inhaled and exhaled with measured slowness, struggling to calm the tension in his body and to ignore the stabbing pain in his forehead.

His blindness was temporary—caused by an old head wound that had damaged his ocular nervous system. He should have expected it; these episodes were brought on by stress and exhaustion. He'd sure as hell had plenty of both today. Two crashes. One in a plane. Another on a scooter.

He felt Lily's hand on his cheek and pulled away.

He didn't want her to know about his vision problem. Gruffly, he asked, "Are you okay?"

"Don't worry about me. You don't look so good."

"Give me a sec."

Her small hand touched his thigh and she made a *tsk-tsk*. "Your trousers are torn to shreds. Our clothing budget on this trip is going to be sky-high."

Praying for light, he opened his eyes and saw nothing but shades of gray. He squinted through the opaque darkness. A while back, a doctor at the VA told him about an operation that might repair the nerve damage. But if it failed, there was a twenty percent change he'd go blind. John wasn't a gambler.

He could deal with these infrequent episodes if he controlled the level of his tension. He had to fight the darkness.

"John?" Her slender fingers laced through his, and she squeezed. "John, you're scaring me."

"Nothing to worry about." Shielding his eyes, he waited for the wiring inside his head to sort itself out. These spells passed quickly. Only a few moments. Just long enough to force him to take a medical discharge from the Marine Corps.

Looking up, he saw the shape of Lily's face. He blinked slowly. Once. Twice. His vision began to clear. Her delicate features swam into focus. "Are you hurt?" she asked.

He wasn't about to share his disability with her. Didn't need her pity. "Let's head back to the hotel."

"Something's wrong," she said.

He pushed himself to his feet. His head was spinning but focus was coming back. He could see the trunks of palms and citrus trees. Thick, leafy ferns. Jagged rocks. The crumpled front wheel of the motorbike. There would be no resale on this equipment. "We'll walk the rest of the way."

It took all his concentration to plant one foot in front of the other as he lurched toward the road. He hadn't had one of these episodes in over two years, had almost begun to believe that he was cured. No such luck.

Lily scampered beside him. "What if they come back?"

He doubted that would happen. "If they'd meant to kill us, we'd be dead by now. The Hummer was a warning. Leave Cuerva."

"I got the message," she said. "And I'll bet I know who sent it. I saw the license plate. GOV 3. It's got to be part of Governor Ramon St. George's fleet."

The governor wanted to scare them off his island? Was he working with Drew Kirshner? The threat to them had to be connected to Robert. But how?

On the road, he set a slow pace. Though he knew the moon was shining brightly, his vision hadn't recovered enough to see details. The earth beneath his feet seemed to disappear into a dull, dark haze.

It was only about a mile to town, and Lily talked the whole way. Mostly about how they could get even with the governor. Casually, she took his arm, and he was silently grateful for her guidance. Damn it, this was all wrong. He should be the one protecting her. Not the other way around.

By the time they got to the well-lit hotel, he had

better clarity and only stumbled once on the stairs leading up to the entrance.

In their room, he collapsed on the red-curtained bed and closed his eyes. What he really needed was a solid eight hours of sleep. But that wasn't likely to happen.

The mattress bounced as Lily joined him on the bed. Though she was quiet, he could feel her eyes on him, asking silent questions that he had no intention of answering. Never before had his temporary blindness interfered with his duties at PPS and it felt like hell, like he was helpless.

Her touch on his arm was as gentle as a nurse. He remembered the weeks after he was wounded. Lying on a hard bed in a military hospital with his head wrapped in bandages, he was completely blind. Not knowing if he would ever see again.

He knew lots of guys who were worse off than he was. Other men in his platoon had died. But he wasn't thinking about them. Despairing, he sank deep into an abyss of self-pity. He couldn't stand the helplessness. John always took care of others. His family. His friends. He wasn't meant to be disabled.

"John?" Her sweetness irritated him. He'd rather hear her bitching about something. "What happened to you when we crashed?"

"The plane or the bike?"

"You know what I'm talking about. I've seen you on the firing range. You're an ace marksman. Tonight, your shots went wild."

"I wasn't that bad."

"You were," she said emphatically. "I held my own fire because I wasn't sure what you were trying to do."

"No point in gunning for a Hummer," he bluffed. "I was trying to scare them off."

"I don't believe you." Her fingers tightened on his arm. "You can tell me what's wrong. I'm your partner."

Logically, she was correct. His disability might put her life in danger, and she deserved to know. But he didn't want to admit to his problem. Especially not here in this hotel room, which was probably bugged.

He sat up on the bed and opened his eyes. The valentine room swam into dull focus. It might help if he had his glasses. He was pretty sure they were in the carry-on bag he'd managed to save in the crash.

Leaving her on the bed, he went to the dresser, where they'd spread the miscellaneous items from their carry-on bags to dry out. The few clothes they'd saved were drying in the bathroom. He found his wire-frame glasses, wiped them off and put them on. His vision was better, but still not great.

Mindful of probable bugs in the room, he turned on the television and went out on the balcony, seeking privacy.

Lily hopped off the bed and joined him. "I didn't know you wore glasses."

"You don't need to know everything about me."

"Please, John. You can trust me."

He saw the vestiges of concern in her frown. She was still worried about him. Damn it. He didn't need a nursemaid. And he sure as hell didn't need to waste any more time feeling sorry for himself. He focused on the business at hand. "We need more information on Ramon St. George and the guy from Denver. Drew Kirshner."

"And how do we get this intel?" she asked. "We lost the computer."

"And the secure phone line," he said. "There's no way to contact Evangeline at PPS."

"How about through the local cops?" she suggested.

"The governor's men tried to run us down with a Hummer. I don't think the Cuerva police are going to roll out the welcome mat."

"We're on our own," she said. "It's just you and me. Stuck on a remote Caribbean island where somebody's trying to kill us."

Though John loved his gadgetry and computers, there was something freeing about having to rely on old-fashioned logic and deductive reasoning. "Let's look at the facts."

"Two assaults," she said. "The sabotaged plane. And the Hummer."

"The methods are very different. The plane crash was sneaky, arranged by an unseen individual who probably wanted to kill us. The Hummer was an in-your-face threat, but they only delivered a warning."

She drew the conclusion. "Two different factions are after us. The governor and somebody else."

"Correct." He appreciated her quick comprehension. "But there is a similarity in both attacks."

"Motive," she said.

"Both the governor and the unknown saboteur want the same thing: to keep us away from Robert Prescott. He's got information or evidence that would harm both of them."

"What kind of evidence?"

"I don't know. Evangeline might have a clue."

"Call her," Lily said. "Just use the hotel phone?"

"It could be tapped," he said.

"What difference does it make?" Her logic was beginning to turn to anger. "Obviously, the bad guys already know who we are. Our undercover identity as lovers isn't fooling anybody."

"But we're still going to maintain that cover."

"Why?"

"Part of the game," he said. "We pretend that we're nothing more than innocent sweethearts. The governor pretends that he's not trying to chase us off his island. Then we see who blinks first."

"That's absurd." She threw her hands in the air. "They know us. We know them. Why can't we just admit it?"

"You want a showdown?" His voice was angrier than he intended. "A face-off in the middle of town with the bad guys at one end of the street and us at the other?"

"I want to find Robert Prescott and get him off this island. That's our mission."

"You don't need to remind me."

"Then be honest with me." She peered into his face. "What happened to you when you pulled your gun? Why are you wearing glasses?"

Why the hell did she keep pushing? He wasn't going to open up and share his whole life. "I'll tell you what you need to know. Nothing more."

"Come on, John. I know I'm a rookie, but we're supposed to be working together."

"It's your job to do what I tell you," he said. "And stop thinking like a cop."

Her sharp gasp told him that his comment struck home. She stepped away from the balcony railing. "You don't think I can handle this."

"I didn't say that."

"You didn't have to. I'm smart enough to read between the lines." Her voice rose in pitch and volume. She was almost shouting. "I can be subtle."

"Go ahead. Announce it to the world."

She turned on her heel. "I'm getting out of here before I say something I really regret."

He watched the angry twitch of her hips as she stalked back into the room and headed toward the door. "Lily, wait. Where are you going?"

"Maybe down to the bar. Maybe I'll pick up some vacationing hotshot from Peoria and show him a real good time." She tossed her head. "Maybe I'll go scuba diving."

He didn't have to see her expression to know how ticked off she was. "It's not safe."

"I can take care of myself."

The door slammed behind her. He ought to run after her, drag her back to the room and give her a stern lecture about not taking unnecessary risks.

But he just didn't have it in him.

LILY BURST OUT OF THE ELEVATOR into the hotel lobby. Adrenaline pumped through her veins. Every muscle in her body was tense. Who the hell did John Pinto think he was? The guru of PPS? The only person who had any smarts?

She'd run into similar attitudes when she was a cop with the Denver PD. Guys who thought they knew it all. Guys who called her Tinkerbell. All she wanted was a chance to prove herself.

Though it was almost two in the morning, the hotel bar was full of slaphappy vacationers. Their laughter and music from a sound system sloshed out into the lobby. But she didn't want a drink, didn't want to make friends with strangers. When she hit this level of frustration and anger, the best solution generally involved physical activity, like going for a marathon jog or a workout at the gym. Martial arts were her expertise, but she wouldn't mind going a couple of rounds with a heavy punching bag. She'd pretend she was taking jabs at John, unloading a sharp left to his sculpted nose, then a right to his stubborn chin. She'd wipe that smirk off his handsome face. Only he hadn't been smirking, hadn't been purposely teasing or trying to make her feel bad.

He'd been hurt when they'd crashed off that bike. He'd been dazed but refused to admit it. Didn't trust her enough to share his pain.

Turning away from the bar, she slipped through the French doors onto the wide patio, which was dimly illuminated by tiki lights. In the shadow of a palm tree, two lovers were kissing and moaning loudly.

Another older couple sat side-by-side near the edge of the patio, holding hands and gazing out to sea. They reminded her of her parents. Calm and loving, her mom and dad seemed complete in each other's company. Lily always felt like a brash intruder on their peaceful life. She never fit into the picture. Not with her small family. Not with friends. And certainly not now.

The way John treated her made her feel like a child who couldn't handle grown-up secrets. His plan to pretend the governor's men hadn't tried to run them down was idiotic. Or was it? Was she too inexperienced to understand how this undercover stuff worked?

As she stepped down the wide steps to the sandy beach where they had danced earlier, she slipped off her shoes. When she'd chatted with Governor Ramon St. George, he must have already known that she and John were from PPS and were here to make contact with Robert Prescott. And when the governor invited her to the mansion? Perhaps that was his plan from the start. To keep her and John where he could watch them.

The guy who had tailed them through town must have been one of the governor's men. Maybe even one of the local cops. How had Robert Prescott managed to offend half the population of the Caribbean? Whatever information he had must be explosive.

The rhythmic lapping of the surf drew her closer to the frothy waves that skimmed the shoreline. Earlier, John had said they couldn't walk on the beach because they were targets. But she'd be safe here.

The hotel wasn't far away, and there were witnesses. She glanced toward a heavyset man in a black-and-yellow patterned shirt. He sprawled facedown across the bar of the beachfront shack with a thatched roof. Though the bartender was long gone, this drunk looked like he was waiting for another round.

Standing in the rising surf, she allowed the cool waves to caress her ankles. Her heels sank deeper in the sand. She kicked her toe, sending up a shimmering arc of salt water. Balmy breezes cooled her face. The island's beauty soothed her anger. This night was close to paradise. So romantic.

And she was here with John—a man with too many secrets. Any kind of relationship with him would be an exercise in frustration. Even though they had a natural chemistry, he was too completely closed down.

Slowly, she walked along the beach at the edge of the waves. What was it that made John so secretive? She knew that he'd grown up on the Navajo reservation in Arizona, but he wasn't the type of man who'd be ashamed of his upbringing. If anything, he was too proud. Arrogant, really. Always thought he was right.

From the trees bordering the beach, she heard the squawk of exotic birds. John could have told her the names and coloration of every bird species. He'd studied all pertinent data about Cuerva.

Lily felt herself beginning to smile as she thought of John and his methodical ways. He'd memorized the map of the island, planned every step of the way. Yet there were those intriguing moments of spontaneity, like when he kissed her on the mouth at the airport in Jamaica.

Thoughtfully, her fingertip traced the line of her lower lip. Some amazing kiss.

Behind her back, she heard splashing. Someone was coming toward her. "John?"

He was close. She could feel him right behind her.

Before she could turn, he crashed down on top of her, knocking her off her feet. Face down in the shallow water.

He jerked her upright and lifted her off her feet. His arms wrapped around her middle and carried her into the waves.

She struggled, jabbing with her elbows, kicking wildly.

After a few steps into the water, he toppled forward. His heavy bulk pressed down. Her face was under the water. For the second time in one day, she was drowning.

He yanked her out of the water, and she caught a huge gulp of air. Her eyes stung. She shook her head.

His mouth was right beside her ear. He growled, "Where is he? Where's Robert Prescott?"

Lily shook her head. Even if she'd known the answer, she wouldn't tell him.

He shoved her down again. Under the water.

Chapter Five

John searched the hotel bar and didn't see Lily among the tourists. Where the hell had she gone? He stalked through the lobby and onto the patio. His vision was almost back to normal, but he still wore the wire-rimmed glasses as he stepped out into the moonlight.

It was almost two o'clock in the morning, and he was tired. All he wanted was to locate his partner, haul her cute little butt back up to the room and grab some sleep. But he couldn't help being struck by the beauty of Cuerva. The white sand. The silver thatch palm trees. And the sea.

Ever since they'd arrived in the Caribbean, Lily had been wanting to stick her toes in the water. A more sensible woman might have been cured of that desire by plummeting into the sea in a plane crash, but he didn't expect common sense from Lily. She was volatile, emotional and spontaneous. The direct opposite of him.

Tramping through sand to the water's edge, he

scanned in both directions. He saw a big man, thigh-deep in the rolling waves, struggling. He had Lily. With a rough jerk, he pulled her out of the water, then plunged her facedown again into the water.

John couldn't take a chance on using his gun. Not with Lily so close. The logical action would be to run silently and fast, catching the attacker. But if he didn't get there fast enough, Lily could be drowned.

John had to stop this bastard. Right now. He yelled, "Hey! What are you doing?"

The big man turned. He was too far away to see anything more than a hulking silhouette against the moonlight shimmer. He shoved Lily down and took off running through the shallow surf.

Now was the time for John to open fire. But Lily wasn't moving. He couldn't waste precious seconds in drawing his gun and still didn't trust his aim.

At the water's edge, he ran fast. His legs churned. The night parted before him as he charged into the water and found her, staggering to her feet.

When he gathered her into his arms, she was limp. Her delicate body collapsed into his embrace. He scooped her up and carried her to the sandy beach.

Her assailant had disappeared into the trees beyond the beach. Good cover for an assassin. He could be armed.

John carried Lily to the thatched-roof hut that had been used as a bar earlier and set her down on the wood-plank floor.

Her short blond hair was plastered across her forehead. Using the tail of his shirt, she dabbed at the water on her face. "I'm…I'm sorry."

"You're okay?"

"I will be. As soon as I catch my breath."

He should have been angry. She'd put herself and their mission in danger, had disobeyed his instructions, had disregarded his advice. But as he looked down into her wide brown eyes surrounded by spiky black lashes, he felt only relief that he'd gotten to her in time. She was going to be all right.

He drew the Glock from his ankle holster. The gun was wet and might not fire properly, but the heft of his weapon reassured him. "Can you run?"

She sat up straighter. "You bet."

"Stay with me. We're going back to the room."

He set a quick pace, dodging across the sand. When their feet hit the patio, they went even faster. The elevator stood waiting and they darted inside. In their honeymoon suite, he locked the door and turned toward her, breathing hard.

Wet as a drenched rat, she turned toward him. "That guy came out of nowhere and grabbed me from behind. This has never happened to me before. I'm good at martial arts. But he knocked me off my feet."

"Did you get a look at him?"

She shook her head. "All I know is that he was big. Huge. I don't think he was really in great shape. Just bulky. If I'd been facing him, I could have taken him."

"Did he say anything?"

"Oh, yeah." She gave a vigorous nod. "This is all about Robert. The guy kept asking me, 'Where's Robert Prescott?' I should have been more prepared, shouldn't have let him get away."

The words tumbled out of her mouth. Apparently, she had recovered. And he was indescribably relieved to hear her chirpy voice.

He pulled her close against him. His mouth silenced hers with a kiss. The heat from their bodies sizzled against their wet clothing. They melted together.

He wanted this woman, wanted to make love to her. Ever since he accidentally kissed her at the airport in Jamaica, he'd been waiting for the next kiss, the next sensual touch.

Her pliant lips aroused him. Her wiry body felt right in his arms. Though they were as different as earth and fire, they were a perfect fit.

Ending the kiss, he stared into her face. An irrational glow flooded over him. His world shifted. Reality was replaced by clarity. True vision. The truth that came from the Universe.

He saw their future together. A whole lifetime unfolded before him. They would share many years. His vision was as pure as the truth learned after meditation in a sweat lodge, and the knowledge rested easily in his heart. His grandfather had been a medicine man, and his clan was known for its strong intuition.

Lily was his destiny. He could have no secrets with this woman. *His woman.* Taking a deep breath, he leaned close to her ear and whispered, "There's something you need to know. Earlier tonight when I was firing blindly, it was because my vision was impaired."

She nodded, encouraging him to continue.

"A long time ago, I was a lance corporal in the Marine Corps. We were on a recon mission in Africa. A land mine detonated, and I took shrapnel to the head. My ocular nervous system was damaged."

"Where?" she asked.

"Keep your voice down. We might have listeners."

"Where?" she repeated more softly.

"Somewhere in Africa. Does it matter?"

"Not the place." Her fingers stroked through his hair. "What part of your skull was hit?"

"Above my right ear."

She touched the scar, traced the length of it through his thick hair. "And this injury causes temporary blindness?"

"When I'm tired or stressed." He didn't like to admit weakness. "It doesn't happen often. Everything goes blurry. Only lasts a few minutes."

"Isn't there some kind of operation?" she asked.

"Yes, but it comes with a risk. Twenty percent of the time, the operation fails. And I'd be permanently blind."

"Is there a less invasive procedure?"

"I tried everything. My injury meant I had to take a medical discharge from the Marines, and I didn't want to quit." Though it went against his nature, he revealed another of his secrets. "I even had the tribal medicine man perform a Bead Chant."

"A what?"

"It's a long saga about a man who lost his vision and then recovered it. It might seem superstitious, but—"

"Not at all. It's smart to try alternative medicine, even though my parents don't think so. It's part of your heritage." Her lips curved. "I'm glad you told me."

"I want you to know me, Lily." It was too soon to tell her about his vision of their long life together. Better not to frighten her with that knowledge.

AFTER A SHOWER, LILY SLIPPED into a sleeveless pink nightgown from her carry-on bag. The cover-up bathrobe she'd intended to wear had been lost in her other luggage, and all she had left was this light cotton gown. Studying her reflection in the bathroom mirror, she pulled up the lace yoke to hide any sign of cleavage. The tips of her breasts poked against the fabric. Oh, swell.

In this sheer gown, it seemed like she was trying to be sexy, which was, most definitely, not the case. Their earlier game of teasing one-upsmanship was over. John's kiss had taken her breath away. Never before had she experienced such a depth of passion and longing.

And now, upon reflection, she felt like the biggest virgin in the world. Totally inexperienced. How was she going to get through the night in the same bed with him? She wouldn't ask John to sleep on the floor or the sofa. Not after the strenuous day they'd had.

If anybody took a less comfortable place to sleep, it should be her. But she was feeling the aches and bruises. And she wanted to prove that she could be cool, calm and controlled.

Her fingers curled around the bathroom doorknob, and she hesitated, gathering her resolve. Sleeping on the same bed didn't mean they had to have sex. Somehow, she had to keep her distance.

She whipped open the door.

He was already in the bed, leaning back against the pillows with his fingers laced behind his head and his eyes closed. He had folded the comforter down and pulled up the red satin sheet to cover the lower half of his body. His chest was bare. His smooth bronze skin made a rich contrast with the crimson sheet. She couldn't see an ounce of fat on his muscular torso. The man was perfect.

Slowly, his eyelids lifted, and his dark gaze glided over her body. Her nerve endings quivered. Her tight nipples brushed against the thin fabric of her gown.

"You're pretty in pink," he said.

She swallowed hard and opened her mouth to respond, but no words came out.

"We can speak normally," he said. "I swept the room for bugs."

"Why didn't you do a sweep when we first got here?"

"I was playing the undercover role. Letting our listeners think we were just a couple having an affair."

"And now that we've been attacked?"

He shrugged. "Maintain the status quo."

"We know that they know." This was confusing. "And vice versa. They know that we know that they know."

"Pretty much."

In her years as a cop, she'd never done anything so complicated. "Did you find bugs?"

"Three," he said. "Even though I don't have my electronic sweep equipment, I'm confident that I got them all. These listening devices weren't sophisticated. The people monitoring us aren't surveillance experts."

When it came to electronics, John was the best. Through PPS, he designed security systems for top-level companies. Here in Cuerva, without access to his equipment, he'd improvised. Glancing around the room, she noticed a chair pushed up against the door from the hallway. Likewise, he'd booby-trapped the French doors leading onto the balcony. His automatic weapon rested on the bedside table within easy reach.

He'd done what he could to secure their honeymoon suite against outside threats. But Lily didn't feel safe. The sexy glow from his dark eyes sent warning quivers up and down her spine. She blurted, "We're not going to sleep together."

"There's only one bed."

"You know what I mean. No sex."

He pulled down the cover on her side of the bed. "I would never rush you."

She hurried across the room and dove under the covers. His nearness was a palpable force—a magnet drawing her toward him. She fought the pull, curling up on the far edge of the bed with her back turned to him. "I'm sure you understand," she said. "Having sex would create a negative working environment."

"I understand."

"I mean, it's unprofessional. And I'm not in favor of casual sex." Or any sex at all. But she wasn't about to admit that she was still a virgin. "I believe in committed relationships, and that could never happen with us. We're too different."

"You never know," he said. "My people used to declare their mate in ritual dances. A young man had to prove himself worthy. The young woman had to declare herself available for courtship. If both families approved, a marriage would take place."

"The final decision was up to the family?"

"Family is important."

Not to her. She couldn't imagine asking permission to engage in courtship. "Are you close to your family?"

"Yes." He turned off the bedside light. The intimacy of darkness surrounded them. "Sleep well, Lily."

Though she couldn't imagine how sleep was possible, her heartbeat slowed. Her breathing calmed. She'd come close to death three times today. Kind of a hectic schedule.

Like feathers on a dying wind, her fears subsided and she fell into a deep slumber.

WHEN SHE WOKE THE NEXT MORNING, Lily found herself sprawled across the queen-sized bed with the red sheets—*all* of the sheets—twined around her in a clumsy cocoon. Apparently, she'd spent most of the night hogging the covers. What else had she done? A quick memory search revealed no further kissing, fondling or embracing. She groped toward the pillows. John's side of the bed was empty.

Squinting against the sunlight that gushed through the windows, her gaze swept the room. He stood at the balcony with one long arm braced against the open French doors. A light breeze ruffled his black hair. He wore khaki trousers. No shoes. No shirt.

Below his rib cage, a nasty-looking bruise darkened his smooth skin. In every other way, he was flawless.

"You're awake," he said.

"Barely." The bedside clock said it was ten minutes past eleven o'clock. "Sorry I took all the covers."

"Sleeping with you is like being in bed with the U.S. gymnastics team."

Made sense. She felt like she'd spent the night doing triple flips. "How long have you been up?"

"Long enough to order breakfast."

When she untangled herself from the sheets, Lily discovered her own set of aches and bruises. Her neck was stiff. The joints in her legs felt like she'd been through a wringer.

There was a knock on the door. "Room service."

When John went to answer, he held his pistol in his right hand. Being armed was a smart precaution, but she wasn't accustomed to such vigilance. Protecting herself had been a lot easier when she was a cop. The danger ended when her shift was over, and the bad guys were obvious thugs and miscreants.

On Cuerva, the danger came from the governor himself. And from Drew Kirshner—the visitor from Denver with shadowy connections to the Russian mob.

The room service person in a white chef's jacket rolled a linen-covered cart toward the table near the balcony. There was something familiar about the set of his shoulders. "Edgar?"

He turned toward her and beamed a huge, white grin. "Top of the morning, Lily." His British accent was far too peppy. "Coffee?"

"Black with two sugars."

As he poured from a carafe, he said to John, "I brought you a little something extra. It's under the tablecloth."

John whisked aside the linen. "A satellite phone. Secure line?"

"The best MI6 can provide."

Mindful of her see-through gown, Lily draped herself in the red satin sheets as she stumbled toward the delicious coffee aroma. Accepting the delicate china cup, she sank into a rattan chair. The sheets puddled around her ankles like an ill-fitted toga.

"Last night," John said, "we missed our connection with Robert Prescott. Have you heard from him?"

Edgar shook his head. "Nary a word. When Robert doesn't wish to be found, he is the invisible man."

"You're right about that." Lily blew on her coffee. "There aren't many people who could manage to disappear for two whole years."

"Quite so." Edgar sat in the chair opposite her and crossed his long legs. "Tell me about your evening."

"The governor's men tried to run us down in a Hummer. The license plate was GOV 3." She narrowed her eyes. "You warned us about Governor

Ramon St. George. Do you have any idea how he's connected to Robert Prescott?"

While he considered the possibilities, Edgar laid a finger across his thick lips. His brow furrowed.

Lily sipped her coffee, savoring the rich flavor and hoping the caffeine would jolt her awake.

"The governor's main concern," Edgar said, "is to maintain his lucrative offshore banking endeavors. If Robert is mucking around in his financial affairs, Governor St. George will not be pleased."

John took a bottled water from the room service cart, screwed off the top and took a sip. "There are over two hundred banking institutions on the island of Cuerva, including two thousand trusts and probably three thousand corporations."

"Wait a minute," she said. "Last night, when we were running around in the town, I didn't see enough office space for all these thousands of businesses."

"Most of them are nothing more than a plaque on the wall or a blip on a computer screen." He glanced toward Edgar. "Ever hear of Kingston Trust and Investment?"

Edgar shook his head. "As you mentioned, there are thousands of these trusts on Cuerva. Even more in the Caymans."

But Lily understood John's reference. Back in Denver, Kingston Investment was tied to a string of murders. Every victim had been part of a blind trust—Kingston Trust—including Nick Warner, who'd been under the protection of PPS when he died. And Peter Turner, who was still in a coma.

Peter was the half brother of Kyle Prescott, Robert's son from his first marriage.

How strange. These murders in Denver might find their solution in the Caribbean.

John said, "According to my research, there are only a handful of substantial bank buildings on Cuerva. One of them is Bank St. George."

"Named for the governor." Edgar rose to his feet. "Any threat to Bank St. George would be sufficient reason for the governor to chase you off his island."

"And sabotage your plane?"

"Possibly."

"But you have doubts," John said.

"My true identity is rather well-protected," Edgar said. "I spend most of my time on Jamaica and seldom visit Cuerva. Few people know of my history with MI6. If they did, I wouldn't have a restful retirement, would I?"

"So we can assume that the person who sabotaged your plane was following me and Lily. Not you."

"Quite likely."

Last night, they had already drawn that conclusion. Two different factions were after them. One was associated with the governor. The other was unknown.

Edgar strode toward the door. "I shall leave you to your breakfast and your secure phone line."

"How can we contact you?" she asked.

"I'll stay in touch, dear girl." He flashed his brilliant white smile and exited. "Do try to enjoy your stay in the Caribbean."

Not much chance of that.

Chapter Six

Checking his wristwatch every few minutes, John filled up on a breakfast of eggs, bacon, papaya juice and coffee, lots of coffee. He also downed a couple of over-the-counter painkillers that Edgar had thoughtfully provided along with their room-service food.

There was no point in calling the PPS offices until twelve o'clock Caribbean time, which would be nine in Denver, but waiting was difficult. He had the thread that might unravel the whole scheme: Kingston Trust and Investment.

He pushed back from the table and looked over at Lily. Slow to waken, she was cute in the morning when her gestures were drowsy and her short blond hair stuck out in spikes. Her mood was contemplative and quiet as she picked bits of yellow pepper and onion from her omelet.

"You're a fussy eater," he said.

"Simple tastes." She nibbled at her bacon. "I could live on mac and cheese."

"But you asked the governor about the recipe for curried goat."

She wrinkled her nose. "I hate to think what they'll be serving at the cocktail party this afternoon."

"Fried cockroaches. Turtle soup. Iguana stew."

"Iguana?" She shuddered. "I'll stick to mangos and papayas."

He glanced at his watch. Evangeline was probably on her way to the downtown Denver office, but he didn't want to talk to her on the cell. He needed her undivided attention, but he couldn't wait any longer. At ten minutes until noon, he punched in the number on the secure phone line.

His call went through to the Prescott Personal Securities receptionist, who was nicknamed Angel though her Gothic clothing looked more like a latter-day vampire, the Angel of Death. "Is Evangeline in?"

"Nope." Angel punctuated the word with two snaps of her chewing gum. In spite of the black lipstick, macabre jewelry and somber clothes, she had a ditzy personality.

He asked, "Will she be in soon?"

"Dunno. She's got a couple of meetings this morning." *Snap, snap.* "It's early, John. Nobody's here but me and Sara Montgomery."

"Did Evangeline leave any messages for me?"

"Um, yeah. Let me see if I can find it."

"It's important, Angel."

"Yeah, yeah. Life and death. Blah, blah."

Grinding his rear molars, he waited. Angel was

the least professional person in their office, but Evangeline insisted that Angel had potential. Potential for what?

"So," she said, "you and Lily. Have you hooked up yet?"

"What?"

"The two of you. Yin and yang. A total match."

He hated when the ditz hit on an accurate perception. "Where did you get that idea?"

"I get it. I get you. Both of you." He heard the shuffle of papers and imagined Angel throwing important messages in the air like confetti. "Opposites attract."

"Let me talk to Sara."

Sara Montgomery's voice was calm and well-modulated, underlining the upper-class background she'd left behind to become part of PPS. "How can I help you, John?"

"I've lost my secure computer and need information. Everything you've got on Drew Kirshner, Kingston Trust and Ramon St. George."

"Hang on. I'll do it right now."

His fingers itched to be typing into his own laptop and doing his own research. But he didn't dare use a computer provided by the hotel; his inquiries could be too easily traced.

She asked, "Have you made contact with Robert Prescott?"

"Not yet."

He knew that Sara had reasons beyond general concern to be worried about Robert. She'd recently become involved with Kyle Prescott.

John asked, "How's Kyle?"

"Waiting for news about his father. Bring him back in one piece, John.

"That's the plan."

"We're still worried about Peter."

Peter Turner, Kyle's half brother, was in the hospital. In and out of a coma. "Any improvement?"

"In one of his lucid moments, he asked for a pen and paper. The first word he wrote was *Sorry.*"

He heard a catch in her voice. Both she and Kyle had suspected Peter of wrongdoing. "His injuries aren't your fault, Sara."

"That's logical, but I still feel guilty. Peter is really trying to help us. The second word he wrote was *Coyote.* I don't know what it means, and he never explained."

John had many associations with the word. According to legend, the coyote was a trickster. That description suited Peter Turner. Though he might be trying to help the PPS investigations, his first loyalty would always be to his father and mother. And to TCM, Tri Corps. Media. That multi-million-dollar business was run by Stephen Turner, the current husband of Robert Prescott's first wife, Olivia.

John had never understood what Robert saw in Olivia, a demanding and volatile woman. Sure, Olivia was attractive and looked much younger than her fiftysomething age. When she wanted to be charming, her emerald eyes glowed. But John had seen her at the opposite swing of the pendulum, snarling with fierce rage or observing with a cold, calculated stare. Lucky for her, Olivia was rich enough that people had to put up with her eccentricities. John was amazed that Robert's son had turned out as well as he had after being raised by such a witch.

"Here's what I've got," Sara said. "Drew Kirshner is associated with TCM and with the other murdered investors in the Kingston Trust. You know how much it would help our investigation to get a list of their names."

"It's a blind trust," he said. Names of investors were strictly confidential.

"Drew Kirshner could be the next victim," she said.

"Or he might be the mastermind behind the other murders." If Kirshner was behind the plane crash and the attack on Lily at the beach, he sure as hell wasn't acting like a victim.

"Could be," Sara agreed. "Here's some other useful info. Kingston's offshore account is located in Cuerva. I've got very little on Ramon St. George. He was educated in Great Britain and appointed governor by the queen."

Which didn't explain why someone was trying to kill them. The answers lay with Robert. "Thanks, Sara."

Angel cut into their conversation. "I found it. The note from Evangeline."

He asked, "What did she want to tell me?"

"It's kind of bizarro." Angel gave a giggle. "Evangeline said to remind you that Robert loves to golf."

"GOLF," LILY MUTTERED AS SHE lined up a putt on the third hole of Cuerva's only course. "I can't believe we're playing golf."

With a precise little tap, she sank the putt.

"You're good," John said.

"My father taught me." The old cliché about doctors playing a lot of golf was true in her case. Both parents loved the sport. Several of their family vacations centered on being near renowned golfing venues. "This is an easy course as long as you keep the ball on the fairways and greens."

The manicured grass was bordered by thick foliage. Any drive that went into the rough could probably be considered lost.

She watched as he missed his putt and glared at his rented putter as if something must be wrong with it. There was nothing wrong with him. In his white knit shirt and khaki trousers, John looked like he'd fit right in on the PGA tour. The man was gorgeous; he'd fit in anywhere.

When she was pretending to be his lover and playing her game of teasing, Lily hadn't hesitated to touch him and snuggle against that firm, sexy chest. Now, she didn't dare come too close. A mere glance at him set her heart racing. She'd never been so turned on, and this wasn't the right time for it. She needed to stay on focus, to prove to John and the rest of the staff at PPS that she had what it took to be a good agent.

He tapped the ball into the hole, lifted his head and scanned the surrounding area. From Evangeline's message about Robert loving golf, they assumed there would be some sort of clue or message revealed if they rented clubs and a cart and played nine holes. So far, nothing.

In less than an hour, they were supposed to attend the cocktail party at the governor's mansion. She climbed into the two-person golf cart beside John. "Do you think Drew Kirshner will be at the party?"

"I hope so. This might be our only chance to see him and the governor together."

"What are we looking for?"

"I wish I knew." A frown creased his forehead. "Kirshner might be the next victim. Or he might be behind all the other killings. We should talk to him about common acquaintances in Denver. People at TCM."

"Like Kyle Prescott." She hopped out of the cart, driver in hand. "And we should ask about Kingston Investment."

"If it comes up in conversation," he said. "We're not interrogating Kirshner."

"I won't act like a cop with a suspect," she promised. "Even though that's exactly what Kirshner is. A suspect. A guy who might be trying to kill us."

"Don't expect Kirshner or Ramon St. George to blurt out a confession."

She glanced toward him. "What if they did? What if they confessed that they were trying to kill us and get their hands on Robert and perpetrate a financial scheme that had already resulted in several deaths? We can't arrest them. Even if we were cops, we're on foreign soil and would have to go through extradition procedures."

"We're private agents. Not bound by the rules." His smile was cool and unintentionally sexy. "We have our own ways of delivering wrongdoers to justice."

"Not the governor." She was genuinely alarmed. "If we grab the governor, it could be an international incident."

"I'm not suggesting that we're above the law," he said. "There are other ways of setting things right. Using PPS contacts, we might arrange a freeze on the governor's offshore banking operation."

Though relieved that he wasn't proposing some kind of vigilante justice, she still wasn't sure how all this worked. For most of her rebellious youth, she'd chafed against the rules.

In their little golf cart with a fringed roof, they drove to the tee for the fourth hole. The foursome ahead of them were finishing up at the green, and they waited.

She returned to the question that had been bothering her. "How do we know we're doing the right thing?"

"Trust yourself. Follow your own moral compass." He rested his hand on her shoulder, setting off a hormonal chain reaction that left her shivering. "You're a good person, Lily. When the time comes, you'll know what to do."

"I'm not so sure." In her life, she'd done some incredibly stupid and hurtful things.

"In the meantime, stick to the mission. Getting

Robert Prescott off this island and back to Denver safely."

She hopped out of the cart, teed up her ball quickly and blasted it straight down the fairway. It was a pretty decent shot, almost to the green.

"Don't move," John said.

She froze with her club in the air. "What is it?"

"Turn around slowly."

With her senses on high alert, she measured the distance back to the cart. Because she was wearing shorts and a skimpy red T-shirt, there was no place to hide her weapon. The Glock was in her oversized purse.

Slowly, she turned. Less than twenty feet away was an iguana. The prehistoric-looking beast glared at her through beady eyes. Beyond ugly, this giant lizard was grotesque.

"See the reddish underbelly?" John said. "This appears to be a rock iguana. A more common species than the endangered blue iguana. According to my reading, they don't usually show themselves. And they almost never attack."

"Almost never?"

"He's a beauty. Seeing him is a good omen."

"Right." She was ready to whack this monster with her golf club.

"The lizard is a symbol of dreams. Where I grew up in Arizona, we'd see lizards sunning on the rocks. Motionless but not asleep. Dreaming."

He took a step toward the iguana and leaned down. "Oh, my God," she blurted. "Don't touch it."

For a long moment, John and the iguana stared at each other. Very softly, he said, "Welcome."

The beast bobbed its ugly head, almost as if nodding. Then it turned and ambled off toward the brush on muscular legs.

Without saying another word, John went to the tee, placed his ball and made a long, excellent drive all the way to the green. His best shot of the day. Apparently, the iguana had brought him luck.

They returned to the cart and she asked, "Do you always talk to animals?"

"They're more honest than most people. Ancestors of that iguana were on this island long before humans came. I respect their wisdom."

His self-assurance comforted her. He wasn't arrogant but certain. Without considering all the myriad alternatives, he knew what he was supposed to be doing.

At the tee for the fourth hole, a tall man stepped away from the shadowy trees, dropped his ball and made a putt. His salt-and-pepper hair glinted in the sunlight. Though Lily had never met him before, she knew this was Robert Prescott.

John approached him first. Their formal handshake turned into a hug. The bond between these two men was apparent.

"I didn't expect to see you until tonight at Pirate Cove," John said.

"And we will meet there at midnight. I wanted to see you now to give you a bit of information. Glad you understood my golf reference."

"Did you speak to Evangeline?"

"Not yet." The brightness in his eyes dimmed. "Only a text message."

John waved her over. "Robert Prescott, this is Lily Clark, formerly a policewoman with the Denver PD. She's one of our best rookies."

She shook his hand, noting that Robert looked a lot like an older version of his son, Kyle Prescott. Blue eyes. Firm jaw. Lanky frame. "I'm pleased to meet you, sir."

"And I will enjoy getting to know you." His British accent, though not as upper-crust as Edgar's, lent authority to his tone. "But not now. We don't have time."

"You have a plan," John said.

Robert nodded. "There's one last thing we need to do before we leave the island."

"What's that?"

He smiled at both of them. "We're going to rob a bank."

Chapter Seven

John would have walked barefoot through hellfire
and brimstone to help his old friend and mentor. But
rob a bank? Committing a major felony wasn't what
he'd expected. Hiding his surprise, he asked, "Bank
St. George?"

"Precisely," Robert said. "We need internal access
to the blind trust funded through Kingston Investment."

"Excuse me," Lily cut in. "Are you serious? You
want to rob a bank?"

"Don't worry. We won't be sauntering out the door
with bags of money tucked under our arms. This theft
will be computerized."

"Then why do we need to be inside the bank to
do it?"

"Security reasons too complicated to explain."

John reminded himself that he could trust Robert,
even though his old friend looked like hell. His face
was drawn. He'd lost weight. His khaki shirt hung
loose around his middle.

These two years on the run had been hard on

Robert Prescott. The best cure would be to get him back to Denver and into Evangeline's welcoming embrace. "We need more explanation," John said.

Robert lifted his chin. "For two years, I've been tracking Clive Fuentes."

"Clive who?" Lily asked.

"I'll explain later," John said.

Robert continued, "A former friend turned into my archenemy. His goal seems to be to destroy me and my loved ones. I'm rather ashamed to admit that I've given up hope of locating Clive. The only way to drive him into the open is to attack that which he considers most dear—his money. The Kingston Trust."

He reached under his shirttail and pulled a thick envelope from the waistband of his trousers. "These are blueprints of the bank and electronic schematics so you can figure out how to bypass the on-site security system."

John weighed the envelope in his hand. "How did you get this information?"

"My MI6 contacts. Old friends like Edgar. But I needed your expertise for this break-in, John. There's no one I trust more."

That deep trust and loyalty ran both ways. John accepted Robert's rationale. The bank robbery was necessary. "Let me see if I have this right. We're going to break into Bank St. George and access the internal computer."

"Correct," Robert said. "Then I will transfer all the funds in the blind trust into my own Swiss account. The total amount is several millions dollars."

A very tidy robbery. "When do we strike?"

"Rendezvous tonight at Pirate Cove. Midnight."

"Not much time." It was already after three o'clock. John assumed that Bank St. George had a state-of-the-art security system, and it would take every minute until midnight to figure his way around the alarm systems. "I'll get started right away."

"Don't forget your cocktail party this afternoon," Robert said.

"Wait a sec," Lily said. "How did you know we were invited to the governor's cocktail party? And why should we go? Everybody on this damn island seems to know why we're here and what we're doing."

"They know that you're here to meet with me," Robert responded. "But I doubt that anyone suspects my intention to rob Bank St. George. You can't let them know that we've spoken. It's vital that you appear to be waiting for me to make contact."

"And how did you know about my conversation with Ramon St. George?" she asked.

"Edgar isn't my only contact on the island. I have other ears. And other eyes." He rested his putter on his shoulder and took a step backward. "Until midnight."

"I have more questions," she said. "Why didn't you meet us last night? What if you get held up again? How can we contact you? Where can we—"

"I'm sorry, Lily. We're out of time." He gave her a wink. "By the way, undercover work suits you. Getting yourself invited to the governor's mansion was very clever. Evangeline told me to expect great things from you."

Robert Prescott stepped away from the manicured putting green into the surrounding trees and vanished. If John hadn't been holding the envelope in his hand, he might have doubted that he'd even seen Robert. His arrival and departure were swift as a cloud crossing the sun. Yet in that moment of contact everything had changed. There was a new purpose to their mission. They were going to rob a bank.

Beside him, Lilly ruffled her fingers through her short blond hair. "Clearly, this is illegal. There's no possible way to cast a good light on Robert's plan."

"It's necessary."

"Yeah? Well, you need to convince me."

She approached her golf ball on the green, lined up the putt and sank it. A good sign, he thought. Even when she was agitated, her reflexes were calm.

He glanced back toward the tee for the fourth hole, where another foursome had just arrived. "We need to go back to the room. I've got to study these schematics."

"You're not listening." She stalked across the green toward him. "Bank robbery is a felony. Even here in Cuerva. I'm not going to go through with this unless you give me a clear reason."

"How about the string of murders in Denver." He went to the cart. "The attacks on us. The plane crash. The guy who tried to drown you last night."

"How are these incidents related to the blind trust?"

John took the passenger seat in the cart, opened the envelope and took out the blueprint. A neat red dot marked the location of the computer system, which was, fortunately, not within a vault. "You drive."

"Who the hell is Clive Fuentes?"

The golf cart jerked into motion, sending a cheerful ripple through the fringed canopy as she did a one-eighty and pointed them back toward their hotel.

"I've never met Clive," John said. "He retired from law enforcement in Britain, probably MI6 like Robert. At one time, they were tight. Clive was instrumental in encouraging Robert to start Prescott Personal Securities."

"How?" she asked. "This is all about finances, right? Did Clive provide some of the up-front capital for PPS?"

"Not necessary. Robert has significant personal wealth. But you're right. This is about money. Clive convinced Robert to invest with him."

"In a blind trust?"

"I don't know the details."

But John clearly remembered the day Robert took off on a commercial flight from Denver to meet up with Clive in his home country, Spain. On the drive to the airport, he'd confided in John, told him that he feared Clive was using his investment money in shady business dealings.

When Robert had stepped out of the car at the passenger drop-off area at Denver International Airport, the sun shone brilliantly on his graying hair. His stride had been strong and vigorous. He'd looked younger than his mid-fifties age, full of purpose. The last words he'd said to John were, "Take care of Evangeline and Kyle."

Turning to Lily, he said, "Two years ago, Robert met up with Clive in Spain, intending to confront him about his misuse of funds."

"What kind of misuse? Fraud?"

"Take a look at what's been happening in Denver over the past couple of months. Land grabs. Oil schemes. Murder."

"And you think Clive is behind all of this," she said. "Do you have evidence?"

"I have faith. I believe Robert."

He couldn't blame her for not accepting their plan at face value. She didn't know Robert Prescott the way he did.

"Two years ago," she said, "what happened when Robert finally confronted Clive?"

"Supposedly, they were both killed in a private plane crash."

"Both of them? So you thought Clive Fuentes was dead, too."

"I thought so." He had mourned the death of his friend and accepted the official verdict. "Evangeline always suspected that Clive had survived. The bodies weren't recovered, and she never gave up hope that Robert was still alive."

"I'm beginning to understand," she said, drawing her own conclusion. "Clive played dead to establish a new identity. And Robert stayed in hiding for two years because he didn't want Clive to retaliate against Evangeline or Kyle. And now Robert has enough information to bring Clive down. All he has to do is lure him out of hiding."

"By robbing Bank St. George." He looked down at the complicated schematics from the envelope. "Clear?"

"As mud."

Lily didn't like the plan. Undertaking such a blatantly illegal maneuver went against her moral grain. The only justification that made sense was that Clive Fuentes was a cold-blooded killer—the mastermind responsible for the murders in Denver and the attacks on them.

How did Ramon St. George figure into this picture? And Drew Kirshner? She waved as they passed another foursome on the golf course. Glancing toward her right, she saw another fringed cart driving on the path at the opposite edge of the fairway, headed toward the tee on the fourth green where they'd met with Robert.

There was only one man in the cart. Before he turned away from her, she noticed something familiar about him. Operating on instinct, she swerved in his direction.

"Where are you going?"

"I know that guy."

John leaned forward and squinted. "Is he the one who tried to drown you last night?"

"I'm not sure."

"Lily, we don't have time to chase phantoms. He's probably just another tourist out for an afternoon of golf."

"Where's the rest of his foursome?"

He shrugged. "Maybe he paid extra to have some privacy. Like we did."

"Look at the back of his cart," she said. "No clubs. That's pretty suspicious."

"You're right." John refolded the blueprint and slipped the envelope into the waistband of his trousers at the small of his back. In a practiced move, he drew his pistol from the ankle holster. "He's headed for the green where Robert disappeared. Catch up to him."

She floored the accelerator, roaring up to the top speed of maybe twenty-five miles per hour. Not exactly a rocket. She could sprint faster than this.

The man in the other cart glanced over his shoulder in their direction then chugged past the fourth green. His heavy shoulders hunched around his thick neck. Where did she know him from? "I think I saw him last night at our hotel."

"He's pulling away."

"I can't go any faster."

The cart ahead of them left the pathway and plunged onto a downhill fairway, cutting past a foursome who were definitely not pleased by the distraction. She stayed on the asphalt, knowing it would be faster than going through the grass. But the other cart was too far away.

She glanced toward John. "You could shoot him."

"I can't do that."

"We're never going to catch up. He's getting away."

"Then we have to let him go," John said.

"This guy is up to no good. He was headed toward Robert."

"Lily, we can't gun down every tourist who looks suspicious."

And why not? If they were going to start robbing banks, they might as well go all the way and start a crime spree, become the Bonnie and Clyde of Cuerva.

The cart they'd been chasing zipped behind a bank of trees. He was hidden from sight.

Leaving the path, Lily drove across the hilly fairway. Without shock absorbers, the cart bounced over every bump. The fringe was swinging wildly. She swooped around a sand trap to the other side of the trees where they found the other cart abandoned. The driver was gone.

Stepping on the brake, she jolted to a halt. Damn, this was frustrating. She smacked the heel of her hand against the steering wheel. Where did she know him from? Why couldn't she place him? She was usually good at remembering faces and names.

When John chuckled, she reacted. "Don't you dare start smirking. This isn't funny."

"An attempted high-speed chase in a golf cart? Come on, Lily. It's a hoot."

At her expense. She didn't enjoy looking foolish. Too often she'd been told how cute she was, how pixielike, how very blond. She restarted the cart and aimed toward the clubhouse. "May I remind you that you're the one waving a gun on a golf course."

"Yeah. Guess I'm an idiot."

And he continued to laugh. Usually, when she made jokes, his response was a slightly amused smile. Now, he was Mister Chuckles. "I don't know why you're in such a good mood."

"Why not? I've seen my friend Robert. He looks tired but he's still in one piece. And we've finally got a plan."

"Do we?"

"First we go to a party where half the people there want to kill us." More incongruous laughter. "Then we rob a bank. Hell of a plan."

In spite of her annoyance, she giggled. "Any idea how we're going to make our getaway? This is a very small island."

"I'm sure Robert has our escape covered."

Which didn't make her feel better. Robert didn't seem to have a firm grasp on personal safety. "That probably means we'll be commandeering a cruise ship."

"Or riding on the backs of sea turtles." He reached over and placed a hand on her bare knee. "You're a good partner, Lily."

That was the kind of compliment she cherished. "Thanks."

"Even though that creep in the golf cart got away, it felt good to be the ones doing the chasing."

She had to agree. The chase—though futile—had been exhilarating. She liked being in charge instead of fending off attacks. When she rested her hand atop his, he turned his palm over and clasped her fingers.

A subtle thrill went through her. They were starting an adventure together. Chasing down bad guys. Robbing a bank.

"I don't really know Robert," she said. "But I have faith in you, John."

He lifted her hand to his lips and kissed her fingertips. "I'll try not to lead you astray."

She didn't believe that for one minute.

FROM THE TREES AT THE EDGE of the fairway, Ted Hawley watched Lily drive away laughing. Laughing at him?

Who the hell did she think she was? With her cute little ass and her perky attitude, she was the one who had failed. She hadn't caught him.

But she had gotten a glimpse of him. Did she recognize him? He couldn't take the chance that she had. He couldn't have his identity revealed.

Reaching into his pocket, he glided his thumb over his badge. It never hurt to show your credentials. Even in a foreign country like Cuerva, cops respected each other. It was a brotherhood.

He should have gotten more promotions with the Denver PD. Should have been on SWAT. He'd trained with those guys. Knew all their methods. He even had the equipment.

He blamed Lily for keeping him down.

It wouldn't happen again.

He'd find another way to track Robert Prescott. Right now, he wanted Lily and her smart-ass boyfriend dead. He'd send them out with a bang. A big bang.

Chapter Eight

The governor's mansion spread across a hillside overlooking the town. The cobblestone driveway surrounded a two-tiered fountain of gleaming white marble. The house itself was three stories of gold-painted stucco, decorated with white Italianate arches and ornate trim around the windows. Two painted iguana statues stood guard beside the door.

Leaving their cab, Lily was glad she'd dressed appropriately for the high-class mansion in clothes she'd bought at the hotel shop—a bronze halter dress with a long, flowing skirt that hid the automatic pistol strapped to her thigh. Not that she was planning for this late-afternoon cocktail party to turn into a shoot-out.

She took John's arm and whispered in his ear. "Remind me. What exactly are we supposed to be doing here?"

"Looking innocent."

They had already discussed their story. Since the governor and Drew Kirshner already knew that John and Lily worked for Prescott Personal Securities, they didn't have to lie about their identity. But they would continue the pretense of being lovers engaged in an office romance that went against PPS rules. If asked about Robert, they'd brush off the inquiry, saying that as far as they knew, Robert Prescott died in a plane crash two years ago.

She smiled up at John. Behind his wire-rim glasses, his expression was even more preoccupied than usual.

While they were locked away inside their hotel room, he'd barely glanced at her. His entire concentration was devoted to memorizing the blueprints and electronic schematics of Bank St. George.

On the ride here, their taxi had gone through the Cuerva business district, and they'd checked out the physical structure of the bank. An impressive building of hewn granite, Bank St. George would have looked at home in any metropolitan city. She'd been daunted by the impregnable appearance. In the back of her mind, she'd been hoping for a tiki hut with tellers.

"Something wrong?" she asked.

"I hope Robert has the necessary equipment to get past the bank's security. A laser cutter. Digitized scanner. Echometer." He frowned. "I've got nothing. Not even a pair of pliers."

"If that's all you need," she said. "We can make a stop at the local hardware store."

Though she'd been joking, he considered her suggestion. "That's not a bad idea. It wouldn't hurt to have a pair of tweezers and a nail clipper. And a couple of aerosol containers of hair spray."

"Hair spray?"

"A fine mist in the air can show us otherwise invisible sensor beams."

She wasn't sure whether she should be reassured by his resourcefulness or worried about how totally unprepared they were for this caper. "Have you ever done anything like this before?"

"When I was a kid."

"You robbed banks as a child?"

"Not quite." When he grinned and ran his fingers through his thick black hair, she saw a hint of the boy he once had been. "My family was poor, and I learned to make-do with what I had on hand. I kept a beat-up junker of a car running with duct tape and paper clips."

Which was far different from breaking into a top-level security system. "After this party, we'll pick up some tools," she said. "Right now, we're supposed to look like we're madly in love."

"Think you can fake it?"

Pretending to be attracted to him was the easy part of this assignment. She'd picked up some fresh clothes for him, too. In his black cotton shirt with white embroidery and black trousers, he looked casual, suave and sexy. "I'll force myself."

At the front entryway of the mansion, they were met by a butler in a white jacket. Behind him was one of the unsmiling bodyguards they'd met the night before. Very possibly, he was one of the men who had tried to run over their motorbike with a Hummer.

When John gave their names, the butler checked

a list, then he smiled broadly. "Welcome to the home of Governor Ramon St. George. You're just in time for the Dance of the Blue-Footed Boobies."

"Of course, we are," she said. *Boobies?* All sorts of inappropriate images ran through her head.

"Part of the Sugar Harvest Festival," the butler informed her. "The booby birds used to nest on Cuerva. But no more. They are protected now on Booby Cay. These dancers dress like the birds. When they touch you, you are guaranteed good luck."

He escorted them through a wide marble corridor toward French doors that opened onto a large shaded patio at the rear of the house. At a glance, Lily took in the spectacular ocean view, the landscaped palm trees and dozens of urns spilling over with bougainvillea and orchids. Exotic and beautiful, but she wasn't here to admire the scenery.

She turned her attention toward the crowd. Though the dress was casual, several of the women were wearing designer sarongs, classy jewelry and expensive sandals. This gathering appeared to be mostly professionals, probably people who worked in the offshore banking business. Lawyers, bankers and financiers. Lily wondered how many of these well-heeled people were involved with Kingston Trust.

The easygoing calypso beat from the four-piece band changed to a more steady drumbeat. Governor Ramon St. George stepped onto the small stage. His voice was loud enough that he didn't need a microphone. "Welcome, ladies and gentlemen. I hope you are enjoying the Tortuga rum and the island delicacies. For your entertainment we offer the Dance of the Blue-Footed Boobies."

Four dancers—two men and two women—wore elaborate feathered skirts and masks with long beaks. With loud squawks, they danced in an elaborate circle while the crowd cheered.

"Interesting," John remarked. "This reminds me of the Navajo kachina dances."

"You have boobies in Arizona?"

"Boobies are sea birds," he said. "But we have roadrunners, magpies and the sacred eagle."

Behind her dark glasses, Lily was able to scan the faces in the crowd with no one the wiser. She spotted a man in an unstructured gray linen jacket who cast a quick glance in her direction. He'd cultivated a light stubble, probably to disguise his double chin. He gave the appearance of a middle-aged creep hanging on to his younger days. Was this Drew Kirshner?

Ramon St. George spoke up again. "The boobies will come among you and give you talismans. Sleep with this lucky token under your pillow tonight and you will dream of your future."

John squeezed her hand and said, "I think the tall male booby has the hots for you."

"Story of my life," she muttered as she took a short, green-tinted glass from a waiter's tray. "I'm a nerd magnet. The sweetheart of the chess club."

"You play chess?"

"And I always win." She sipped the dark liquid. Sweet but with the kick of Tortuga rum, this was the kind of drink that slid down easily, then knocked you flat.

The tall booby stalked toward her, hopping on one foot and then the other. In spite of the strange dance movements, there was something familiar about the way he moved. When he came closer, she braced herself. Resting his beak on her shoulder, he whispered in a haughty British accent, "Good afternoon, Lily."

It was Edgar. She couldn't help but laugh as she felt him slip a package into her oversized purse.

"Tools," he said before he started squawking like a booby and flapped on to the next lady in the crowd.

Was there any disguise Edgar couldn't do? In the short time she'd known him, he'd been a Rastafarian, a pilot, a busboy and a booby. His ability to effortlessly change persona was somehow reassuring. Edgar was a skilled MI6 professional when it came to espionage. She could only hope that Robert Prescott was equally well prepared.

The man in the gray linen jacket approached them. His gait was measured and a bit stiff, almost like he was wearing a girdle. "I know you two," he said. "I'm Drew Kirshner. You're from Denver, aren't you?"

John shook his hand as he gave their names and added, "We work for Prescott Personal Securities."

"We're here on vacation," Lily said. "It's kind of a secret. You know, there are all these silly rules about employees dating."

Kirshner rubbed the stubble on his chin and gave a knowing nod. "I bet you're a rule-breaker, Lily."

"Like you?"

"Not me. I'm just a boring businessman."

With connections to the Russian mob. "I doubt that you're boring. What brings you to Cuerva?"

"Investments."

In Kingston Trust? "Offshore banking? I'm not in that tax bracket, but I find high finance so very interesting. What can you tell me?"

A frown deepened the lines around his mouth, and she could tell that he wasn't buying her innocent act. He turned toward John. "I've never actually used the services of PPS, but I did know Robert Prescott. Tragic about what happened to him."

"Tragic," John echoed.

If she'd still been a cop, Lily would have locked Kirshner in an interrogation room and hammered at him until she got the information she needed. However, as John kept reminding her, she wasn't a cop. She needed to be subtle, to find out if Kirshner was a potential victim or if he was the person who hired someone to attack them.

"I know this sounds crazy," Kirshner said, "but I've heard rumors that Robert Prescott might have survived that plane crash."

"Not a chance," John said. "Robert was deeply in love with Evangeline. If he were still alive, he'd be with her. And with his son, Kyle. Do you know him?"

"We've met." When he turned to take a rum drink from a waiter's tray, the motion was stiff. He gave a grunt and flexed his shoulders. "Back problems."

"An accident?" she asked.

He hesitated before saying, "An old skiing injury."

She had the impression that he was lying but didn't know why. Was he the next victim or a criminal? Had he been beaten or had he strained a muscle while attacking someone else?

Prior investigation had linked Kingston Trust and Investment with Tri Corps. Media. Lily pointed the conversation in that direction. "Kyle's half brother, Peter, is still in the hospital. That's going to cause some problems for TCM. Have you ever worked with them?"

"Who hasn't?" Kirshner gave a harsh laugh. "TCM has its fingers in a lot of pies. Oil deals. Land development. You name it."

Murders for hire? Though the principals at TCM had been cleared of suspicion, there was still a link. "They've also had some very messy dealings, starting with the murder of Nick Warner, the movie star."

"I heard about that."

When Kirshner took a long sip from his rum drink, she wondered if he was covering his expression, trying to look innocent. She pushed, "Did you ever meet Nick Warner?"

"You ask a lot of questions." His features sharpened. "Were you a cop before you went to work at PPS?"

"Yes." Damn it. She wasn't being subtle enough.

"One of Denver's finest," John said.

"That's why you look familiar. A policewoman," Kirshner said. For the first time in their chat, he turned directly toward her, face-to-face. "I probably saw you at one of the fund-raisers for the Denver PD. I'm a big supporter."

Though his statement wasn't in the least suspicious, his mention of cops and fund-raisers tickled her memory. Drew Kirshner hung out with Denver cops and had made a point of mentioning that connection. Why?

As John took over the conversation, she listened with only half an ear. Had Kirshner been trying to tell her something? Was this some kind of subtle threat?

The answer appeared in a visual image. Thick neck. Heavy shoulders. Angry scowl.

In a flash of insight, Lily knew the identity of the man they'd chased across the golf course. He was a cop from Denver. Not from her precinct but close. And he held a grudge against her.

JOHN COUNTED THE MINUTES UNTIL they could reasonably leave the cocktail party. They'd made contact with Kirshner and waved at the governor. If luck was with them, their assignment tonight would be successful and they'd be off this island before dawn. He didn't want to consider the alternative.

At least, he didn't need to worry about dinner. He'd made a full meal of the various fruits, jerked pork and spicy appetizers. The Johnny cakes reminded him of Navajo fried bread. Lily—the picky eater—had stuck to the breads and avoided the more exotic flavors.

From his viewpoint, the most positive aspect of the cocktail party was their pretense of being lovers. He had free license to rest his hand on the small of her back, to occasionally kiss her cheek, to pull her hair off her forehead. Her wispy blond hair felt soft as downy feathers. Usually, he didn't care for short hair on women, but Lily changed his mind. The curve of her skull and the delicate arch of her neck were in perfect proportion.

He liked the way she responded to his caresses. Whenever he touched her, her muscles rippled beneath her fine skin. He couldn't help thinking about more intimate touches. A time when they would be alone.

But not tonight.

As they headed toward the exit, Governor Ramon St. George placed himself in front of them.

John withdrew his hand from Lily's shoulder; he needed to be sharp for this encounter with the man who had sent his men to chase them off the island. Though his method was crude, Ramon was no fool.

John forced a cordial smile. "We appreciate your hospitality, Governor."

"The pleasure is mine, John Pinto." He circled them like a shark, using his large body to separate them from the others. The governor's coral shirt contrasted his dark skin. The color and pattern should have been a good example of festive island wear, but Ramon St. George made it look sinister.

They stood at the edge of the landscaped bluff overlooking the town and the ocean beyond. Ramon's rich voice was low. "Stand here with me and watch the sunset. At the very moment when the sun falls below the horizon, there's a flash of green."

"The color of money," John said.

"American money. What did you think of my speech?"

The governor had talked for a few moments about his lofty aims for improving the lives of the people of Cuerva, whose ancestors were pirates and escaped slaves. He listed the many improvements that came with the arrival of offshore banking and finance.

John related the governor's speech to his own people. "My tribe, the Navajo, was one of the last to establish a casino on the reservation. The increased revenue and employment opportunity has helped many people. But there has also been an increase in crime and addiction."

A heavy frown creased Ramon's brow; he hadn't really been asking for criticism. "Wealth and power are not always corrupt."

"Not always." John had a hell of a lot more to say. He wanted to tell this prideful man that he was on the wrong side, that he was being used by a criminal mastermind. But he bit his tongue. Now was not the time to start conflict.

"Perhaps you should meet the captain of my police force." Ramon gestured over his shoulder toward a very dark-skinned man in a crisp khaki uniform. "You and Lily have something in common with him because you work for a bodyguard service. A type of law enforcement."

"We're on vacation," John said.

"Are you?" Though his eyes narrowed, Ramon hid his hostility well. "Why do you come to my party armed?"

John met his gaze. "We had a bit of trouble last night."

"Did you file a report with the police?"

Lily inserted herself in the conversation, beaming a smile at both of them. "We didn't want to bother with paperwork, Governor. We'll be leaving the island tomorrow morning."

"Tomorrow?" He gave a pleased nod. "But you mustn't go before my housekeeper gives you the recipe for curried goat."

"Absolutely," Lily said. "Can't wait."

In that respect, they were on the same page. Ramon wanted to get rid of them, and John couldn't wait to leave Cuerva.

"Now you must enjoy the sunset," Ramon said.

The glowing sun had colored the skies and clouds in exotic shades of pink and gold. At the instant when the last bit of the sun dipped below the Caribbean, a thin line of green split the horizon.

Lily gasped. "That's fantastic."

A natural phenomenon of reflection and air particles, but John had to agree. Cuerva was a tropical paradise, unfortunately corrupted by greed and the illegal dealings of Clive Fuentes.

He and Lily quickly took their leave. The minute they got into the cab, she started chattering like one of the multicolored island parrots. "When I was talking to Drew Kirshner, I remembered something. I think I know who—"

He placed his finger across her lips and nodded toward the cab driver who had been waiting at the front of the mansion to pick up his fares. At this point, it was best to suspect everyone. "Tell me when we get to our room."

She leaned back against the seat and groaned. "I really want to talk."

"Maybe I can think of something better to do."

"Like what?"

Her tone was a challenge, and he responded. All night, they'd been touching and teasing. He was ready for more, a lot more.

Holding her chin in his hand, he tilted her face up and tasted her lips. The lingering sweetness of Tortuga rum mingled with her own exotic flavor.

She gave a surprised little moan, then she pounced. She was on his lap. In his arms. Her golden-brown eyes peered into his before she kissed him back. A long, thorough kiss. It was everything John had hoped for. He knew that she wanted him as much as he wanted her.

When they broke apart, they were both breathing hard. "You've done this before," he said.

"Not so much."

He glided his hand down the slender curve of her waist. "I want to make love to you, Lily."

Her eyes welled with tears, and she shook her head.

He didn't understand. They were obviously hot for each other. "What's wrong?"

"Nothing."

With his thumb, he wiped a single tear from her cheek. "You can tell me."

She buried her face in the crook of his neck as if she couldn't bear to look at him. In a very small voice, she said, "I'm a virgin."

Oh. Damn.

She threw her face to the crook of his neck.
She couldn't bear to look at him in a very small voice, she said, "I'm a virgin."
Ten James

Chapter Nine

Logically, John couldn't believe it. Tough, smart, competitive Lily Clark was a virgin. How was that possible? The woman had been a cop. She'd traveled and lived a full life. How the hell had she managed to remain…untouched?

As she sniffled against his chest, he patted her shoulder. "It's okay, Lily." He couldn't believe he was saying this. "There's nothing wrong with being a virgin."

"I know." Her voice quavered. "But does it change your mind about making love to me?"

"I still want you," he admitted. How could he not? The friction of her body on his lap had him fully aroused. "Just not in the same way."

"I knew it." She sat up straight and glared. "I suppose you want to be 'just friends.'"

In the blink of an eye, she'd gone from weepy to ticked off. He would never understand this woman. Talking a mile a minute, she continued, "You think I'm frigid. Or some kind of freak. You don't want anything to do with me. Is that about right?"

"Hell, no." What made her think her virginity was a negative? "Have other men reacted that way?"

"I haven't told other men," she said archly.

"I guess that makes me the lucky winner? How come?"

"You were honest with me about your head injury. It's only fair for me to tell you my secret." She jabbed her forefinger into his chest. "Now it's your turn. How does my, um, condition change the way you feel about me?"

"You want the truth?"

"Always."

"Before you told me," he said, "I wanted to throw you down on a bed and take you. Down and dirty. Hot and sweaty. That's what I wanted."

She swallowed hard. "And now?"

He slid his hand behind the nape of her neck. "I want to make love to you slowly. To teach you the pleasures of your body." With his thumb, he traced the shell of her ear. "Starting here with your pink, sensitive earlobe." His hand slipped lower. "To your throat." He cupped her breast. "All the way down to the warm place between your legs. I want to show you the full satisfaction of being with a man."

Her jaw dropped. She didn't seem to be breathing. Her eyes opened so wide that he could see the whites all around her pupils. Great. He'd thrown her into shock.

"Lily?"

"Okay." Her tongue darted out to moisten her lips. "Yes, John. I want that, too."

He enfolded her in his arms, and she shivered against him. These tremors had nothing to do with the balmy island temperature. She was excited. And so was he. Her virginity and the idea of taking her to a new level of fulfillment gave him a lot to consider.

He forced his mind to switch gears. "For right now," he said, "we have other matters to attend to."

"Agreed. And our plans had better work out well." She climbed off his lap. "I don't want to die a virgin."

Their cab pulled up in front of their hotel. Arm in arm, they walked up the stairs toward the entrance. Dusk had settled over the palm trees. On the beach behind the hotel, the calypso band had already started to play.

Though he was hyper-aware of Lily, John couldn't indulge in fantasies about the sexual pleasures that lay ahead of them. Tonight, they were robbing a bank. He needed to get back to their room and spend more time with the schematics for Bank St. George before they met with Robert.

In the elevator, she cleared her throat and tossed her head. He could tell that she was going through a similar struggle to ignore their attraction and focus on their mission. "At the governor's party," she said, "the big booby was Edgar. He slipped some gear into my purse."

"Good. We need all the help we can get." Belatedly, he remembered their earlier plan to go to a shop where they sold items he might use in the break-in. "We should still pick up a few things, especially the hair spray."

"We'll have to go down the street and into town,"

she said. "The hotel shop doesn't have much of a se-
lection in toiletries."

When the elevator doors opened on the sixth floor,
neither of them got out. Instead, he pressed the lobby
button. As they descended, he checked his wristwatch. Almost eight o'clock. There wasn't much
time to prepare.

With Lily at his side, he exited the hotel as quickly
as he'd gone inside. Mentally, he was making a list
of common household items that could be used in a
high-tech break-in.

They were almost to the street when an invisible
heat wave washed over his back. His senses prickled.
Something was about to happen. In the next instant, he
heard the explosion and turned back toward the hotel.

A burst of orange flames shot from a gaping hole
on the sixth floor. Their honeymoon suite had been
blown to hell.

John took her hand. They raced through the other
spectators who stared and shouted. Others fled from
the hotel. The balmy island scene became a wild
melee. He heard a woman screaming about terrorists.

John headed toward the beach and the shelter of the
tropical forest. Behind the thatched-roof tiki shack
used as a bar, he ducked down. Lily was beside him.

"Our room," she said. "If we'd gone inside,
we'd be toast."

Someone had set a bomb with a remote switch
and watched as they'd entered the hotel. At the moment when they should have been inside the room,
the bomb was detonated.

"The question," he said, "is whether we should talk to the authorities. Or go into hiding and try to meet Robert at midnight."

"The police will be looking for us," Lily said. "And the people from the hotel."

"I'm not sure we can hide." This island was too damned small; he doubted they could evade all the people who would be looking for them. Unless they dealt with the search, their chances of remaining unnoticed were slim to none.

He heard the approaching sirens and prayed that no one else had been injured or killed in the blast that was meant for them.

"I think I know who did this," Lily said in a quiet voice. "When I was talking to Drew Kirshner at the party, he mentioned being a supporter of the Denver police. The way he looked at me seemed like a threat, and I remembered a cop I used to work with. His name is Ted Hawley. Big guy. Thick neck."

"Like the guy we chased in the golf cart," John said. "You recognized him?"

"I'm pretty sure." Though not one hundred percent certain, Lily had been thinking about Ted Hawley since her chat with Kirshner. "I think Kirshner hired him. Hawley has gotten in trouble before for moonlighting as a bouncer."

"I thought it was okay for cops to have part-time jobs."

"Not when they beat somebody half to death. If Hawley hadn't been a cop, he'd be in jail."

From the other side of the tiki shack came a

chorus of chaotic shouts punctuated by sirens from fire trucks and police cars. The heavy odor of smoke hung across the white sands. Only a few months ago in Denver, she'd almost been incinerated when somebody lobbed a fire bomb into the apartment of Cassie Allen, another PPS agent. She remembered the searing heat, the blinding smoke and the sudden rush of panic. Could Ted Hawley have been responsible for that explosion?

He represented the worst type of police officer—too eager to pull his weapon and settle disputes with his own brand of sadistic violence. "I had a run-in with him. My precinct was playing a basketball game with Hawley's, and I was hot. Making all my layups and three-pointers."

"You play basketball?"

"Just because I'm short, it doesn't mean I can't shoot," she said. "Hawley was guarding me, and I was making him look bad. He's a big, clumsy oaf and I could dribble around him. Easy."

"You outscored him," John said.

"It gets worse." She sank onto her knees in the sand. "He blocked me with an illegal forearm. And I took him down. A simple karate move. Nothing special. But Hawley fell flat on his back on the hardwood floor and got the breath knocked out of him."

In spite of the horrifying confusion erupting from the hotel, John grinned. "I can see how the guy might hold a grudge against you. What makes you think he'd blow up our hotel room?"

"Hawley's life ambition is to join SWAT. He's

too dumb to qualify on the written tests, but he loves playing with explosives."

Added to the other noise, she heard the whir of a helicopter. A spotlight swept across the shoreline.

"I doubt we can escape," John said.

"We could hide. Robert Prescott has managed to stay hidden."

"He has resources. He could be anywhere. Maybe even offshore on a boat." John unfastened his ankle holster. "We've got nothing. Every cop on the island is going to be looking for us. We might as well turn ourselves in."

She nodded. "We're obviously the victims here. We shouldn't have any problem."

"Yeah, right," he said under his breath. "Assuming the Cuerva cops are good guys."

He had a point. Though Lily firmly believed that most police officers weren't corrupt, she had Ted Hawley as an example of the opposite. "I met the police chief at Ramon St. George's party. He seemed reasonable."

"Even a reasonable cop won't let us carry concealed weapons," John said. "We'll stash our guns and that handy little package from Edgar under the floor of this hut and come back for them later."

She removed her own holster. "I don't like being unarmed while Hawley is at large."

"Can't be helped." He removed the money belt he wore around his waist. "The bank schematics are in here. I'm going to leave them with the guns."

"Good plan. I'm pretty sure the cops would have

questions about why you were carrying around the blueprints to a bank."

They slid the guns and the envelope under the wood floor of the hut. John helped her to her feet. "Let's get this over with."

THE TWO-STORY CUERVA POLICE station was typical of law enforcement facilities all around the world. The center area was a bullpen with scheduling charts, whiteboards, file cabinets and several desks—each held a computer terminal and a towering stack of paperwork.

Lily would have felt right at home if she hadn't been wearing handcuffs. She and John had been sighted immediately at the hotel and quickly taken into custody. The arresting cops had escorted them into a standard interrogation room with a scarred wooden table and a window that was a mirror on the inside.

One of the officers—a wiry black man with fine features—looked enough like the police chief that they could have been brothers. He pointed to two chairs on the opposite side of the table facing the mirror. "Take a seat, if you please."

His partner was more sloppy and less polite. He pushed a fat forefinger into John's chest. "That means you, big guy. And the pretty little lady."

Standard procedure was to separate suspects. Lily considered the fact that she and John were still together to be a good sign. "Please take off the cuffs," she said.

"Oh, poor baby," the sloppy cop said with a sneer. "Are them handcuffs uncomfortable?"

"There's no need for them," she pointed out. "You have us under arrest."

"We haven't been arrested," John corrected. "We haven't been told what crime we're charged with."

"Isn't it obvious?" His Jamaican-sounding accent was musical but his tone was hostile. "Didn't you hear the big boom? Baby, didn't you see the fire?"

"It was our room," John said. "Somebody attacked us. Not the other way around."

His logic fell on deaf ears. The cops exchanged a glance and shrugged.

John tried again. "At least tell me what we're suspected of."

"Don't have to charge you. We can hold you forever and a day. Yeah, baby. You're terrorists."

Bad news. She hadn't considered the possibility that they could be held as enemy combatants. Terrorists. They could be in deep trouble.

Putting aside her fears, she tried to sound reasonable. "Just uncuff us. We can't escape."

"Do I know this? Do I believe you, baby? You might be planning to explode the whole police station."

"With what? You frisked me." A particularly humiliating procedure with his hands lingering on her breasts and her butt. "I'm clean."

Her shoulders ached from the unnatural restraint of having her wrists fastened behind her back. Plus, she knew that taking off the cuffs showed her and John in a different light. Unshackled, they appeared less criminal. "Please."

The clean-cut officer gave the order. "Remove their handcuffs."

His partner came around behind her back. Leaning close to her ear, he whispered, "Bend over, baby."

Fighting for control, her muscles tensed. She wanted to go on the offensive, to knock this so-called cop off his feet. But she wasn't a fool. Their goal in this interview was to cooperate and be released before midnight. With her wrists free, she laced her fingers together and sat at the table.

John took his place beside her. Under the table, his knee pressed against hers. His nearness reassured her; she hoped they wouldn't be separated. The Cuerva jail didn't look like a hellhole, but she didn't want to be locked up alone.

The chief of police entered the interrogation room. Immediately, Lily gave him a huge smile and reminded him of their prior meeting. "It's good to see you again, my friend."

"I am not your friend." He nodded to the officer who looked like his twin. "Good work in apprehending the terrorists."

"We're not terrorists," John said quickly.

"This remains to be seen.

"Nobody had to apprehend us because we willingly turned ourselves in to your officers. Believe me, Chief, we want to find the person who bombed our room as much as you do."

Hands clasped behind his back, the Chief paced in front of the mirror. "Show me your passports."

Lily winced. "My passport was in the room. It was lost in the explosion."

"How convenient," he said. "How did you get to Cuerva?"

"Private plane from Jamaica," John said.

"But we have no record of this plane. You didn't pass through customs."

"There was a mishap," John admitted. "The plane went down before landing."

"Yet you failed to report this incident. I find this circumstance to be suspicious." He rested both hands on the table and leaned across. "Why are you here? What are your intentions?"

"Vacation."

The chief turned his dark beady eyes on Lily. "Why?"

"We haven't been sneaking around," she said. "We were staying in the honeymoon suite at the hotel, enjoying your beautiful island."

"Lies." He stepped back and nodded to the ill-suited cop who kept calling her baby. "Take her into another room."

"No," she said. "I want to stay here."

"You have no right to make demands. You may go peacefully or not."

"Don't threaten her." John rose to his feet. His presence expanded to fill the room. "We haven't broken any laws."

The chief gestured to his officers. "Take her."

Lily felt herself being yanked to her feet. Her hip banged against the edge of the table, and she gasped sharply. From the corner of her eye, she saw John begin to move. His action was swift but so precise that it almost seemed like slow motion.

He tore the cop's hands away from her and spun him around. With one jab to the chin, John knocked the man unconscious, then turned on his partner who was attempting to draw his gun.

With a well-aimed kick, John disarmed the second cop.

The interrogation room wasn't large enough to contain John's furious energy. He pinned the police chief against the wall.

"We'll cooperate," John said calmly. "We want you to apprehend the bomber. Understand?"

The chief nodded dumbly.

John continued, "It's your job to treat me and Lily with respect. We aren't criminals. We're victims."

She had never seen a man who looked less like a victim. John had kicked ass. He'd been amazing. A force of nature. In hand-to-hand combat, he might be better than she was.

The door to the interrogation room flew open, framing the huge shoulders of Governor Ramon St. George. "I demand the release of these two prisoners into my custody."

The police chief peeled himself off the wall and straightened his spine. "I have reason to believe they are terrorists."

"Nonsense." The governor scoffed. "We have no terrorism on Cuerva. This is a safe place for tourists and for business."

"But the explosion—"

"An accident."

Lily almost laughed. What kind of accident could blow up a hotel room?

"I must investigate," the police chief said.

"Of course," Ramon said smoothly. "And you will find that this explosion was the result of faulty wiring. The fire is already out. No one was hurt."

Lily knew she was witnessing Cuerva politics in action. The governor needed to encourage tourists with fat wallets and businesses with a lucrative agenda. His plans for the island didn't include a terrorist threat.

The cop on the floor rolled to his stomach and groaned. "My head. Oh baby, my poor head."

When she looked away from him, her gaze linked with that of Ramon St. George. His expression was unreadable as he said, "You will come with me. Both of you."

Though Lily hadn't wanted to spend time in the Cuerva jail, she had the feeling that they'd just been pushed out of the frying pan and into the fire.

Chapter Ten

There was no excuse. John knew he'd made a serious mistake at the police station. He'd lashed out like a street fighter, and the knuckles on his right hand hurt from cracking the jaw of the first cop. The guy deserved it; he'd been pawing at Lily all night, acting more like a pimp than a police officer. But, damn it, there was no excuse.

He'd blown any chance at sympathetic treatment from the police chief. Not that he'd expected to be awarded a medal. But he'd hoped they would be able to tell their story and be released. Being in the custody of the governor was a hell of a lot more dangerous. Ramon St. George ran this island. If he decided that John and Lily were too much of a problem, he could make them disappear, turn them into bite-sized snacks for the local sharks.

Flanked by the governor's personal bodyguards—well-armed, muscle-bound professionals who wouldn't fall for a sucker punch—John and Lily were directed into the rear of a black stretch limousine.

Lily sat close beside him, clutching her purse, which she'd demanded be returned to her. When he glanced down at her, he saw determination in the set of her jaw. But she couldn't hide the flicker of fear in her eyes.

The governor and one of his guards sat on the bench beside them. Ramon St. George turned on the overhead light so he could see them clearly. His full lips twisted in an angry scowl. "I was warned about you, John Pinto. I was told that you came here to make trouble. Why?"

There was no point in sticking to the cover story that he and Lily were lovers seeking privacy. The explosion in their room had literally blown any pretense of innocence. But how much did Ramon know about their mission? John opted for the truth. "We were supposed to meet a friend."

"Robert Prescott." Disgust colored Ramon's voice. "Why are you meeting him?"

"I've known Robert for years," John said. "His wife sent us to find him and bring him home."

"But we failed," Lily added. "We had a meet scheduled last night at Pirate Cove, but Robert never showed."

"I know," Ramon said.

"I thought you might," John said. "Your men were following us. They ran us off the road."

Ramon didn't bother to deny the accusation. "They told you to leave the island. Good advice. You should have listened."

The bodyguard who sat beside Ramon shifted his weight. Broader than a linebacker, he held his gun loosely in his left hand. His right hand folded into a huge fist. He wore heavy gold rings on all four fingers. Enough hardware to cause serious damage in a fight.

"Where are you taking us?" John asked.

"Airport. I want you off this island."

Though common sense told John to agree, he wouldn't abandon Robert. Not after two years of waiting for him to surface. "We have a problem. Lily's passport was blown up in the room."

Ramon frowned as he considered. Her lack of passport was a problem for any legitimate transportation. "I wanted to keep this quiet."

Too late for that. "Pretty hard to keep an explosion quiet."

"It was an accident," he said sticking to the explanation that wouldn't malign the reputation of his island paradise.

"An accident arranged by one of your men?"

"If I wanted you dead, I'd take care of that matter without destroying property."

The good news was that he apparently didn't want them dead.

"Explaining your demise would present problems. Too many people know you're here." The governor bared his white teeth as he leaned toward John. "But don't get too comfortable."

And that was the bad news. If their deaths turned out to be expedient, the governor wouldn't hesitate.

Lily said, "If *you* didn't set the bomb, who did?"

"A professional. The fire was minimal, and most

of the damage was limited to your suite. Repairs will be done in a matter of days."

As if the explosion had never happened. The visitors to the island could go back to having fun, and the offshore banking business could continue uninterrupted.

"But why?" Lily asked. "Who's trying to kill us?"

"Robert Prescott has many enemies."

Ramon barked a change of directions to the limo driver. They were going to the governor's mansion.

"Tomorrow," he said, "my people will arrange for a replacement passport and you'll be flown to Jamaica and escorted to a commercial flight back to Denver. Tonight, you stay at the mansion where I can keep an eye on you."

"Are your guests still there?" Lily asked. "Because we'd be happy to pop in and reassure people that we weren't injured. And that the explosion was an accident."

"Good public relations." He raised an eyebrow, assessing her. "But I don't trust you, Lily."

"Me?" Her voice went up. "Why not?"

"I'm a politician. I know when people are lying, and you're very good at sliding around the edge of the truth. Not so with John Pinto."

John met the governor's scrutiny with a straightforward glare. "What are you implying?"

"You're an honest man," Ramon said. "Look here in my eye. You can see that I'm not playing games. If you don't cooperate with me, you will be a dead but honest man."

John had expected as much. Unfortunately, he had no intention of leaving Cuerva without Robert.

THIS TIME, WHEN THEY ENTERED the gold stucco mansion, they weren't greeted at the door as guests. The limo pulled around to a side entrance. One of the bodyguards clamped his hand around Lily's upper arm. The other guard took John. They were rushed inside and up the staircase to a bedroom on the second floor. Though the windows faced the front of the house, she could hear laughter and conversation from the back patio.

For a moment, she considered screaming, calling for help, but she held back. Their best chance for getting off this island alive was to cooperate with Ramon St. George.

Dropping her purse on the bureau, she looked around the large bedroom. Cream-colored walls stretched to high ceilings with a small, sparkling chandelier light fixture. The furniture was an ornate Colonial style in a rich cherry wood. Ornate brocade draperies covered the two arched windows. She couldn't have asked for a more tasteful prison.

The bodyguard holding John had not released his grip. The governor and the other bodyguard stood in the doorway. "You'll be watched," Ramon said. "Don't try anything."

"We won't," she promised. "We're more than ready to leave Cuerva."

"Very wise." He turned to the bodyguard beside him and gave a nod. "There's one more thing…"

The bodyguard holding John made a move. He pinned John's arms behind his back.

Instinctively, Lily took a step toward him. Ramon caught hold of her arm and spun her around to face him. His dark eyes were cold as black ice. "Don't interfere."

The hell she wouldn't. "What are you doing?"

"At the police station," Ramon said, "John Pinto attacked my officers. I can't allow that deed to go unpunished."

The second bodyguard shrugged off his jacket, flexed his hand and pulled his fingers into a fist. His heavy gold rings shone in the light from the chandelier.

"Wait." She couldn't stand idly by and allow her partner to be beaten. "Ramon, this is barbaric. You can't do this."

"I am the governor." He anchored her in place, holding both arms. "I am the final authority."

Which meant he could do any damn thing he wanted. He'd ordered his men to follow them, to run them down on a back road. He'd yanked them from the police station. On Cuerva, Ramon St. George was in charge.

Though she knew there was no point in physical resistance, she couldn't stay silent. "You can't do this. You're a civilized man."

"Usually." He gestured to his bodyguard.

The big man drew back his arm. His first blow was straight into John's gut, doubling him over.

Cringing, she felt the pain—almost as much as if she'd been the one being beaten.

The second blow was to John's jaw. His head

snapped back, but he didn't lose consciousness. And he didn't cry out. When the two bodyguards stepped away from him, John was unsteady on his feet but still standing.

"Consider this a warning," Ramon said. "Do as I say and no further harm will come to you."

Releasing her, he stepped outside with his bodyguards and closed the door.

She rushed across the room to John. "Are you all right?"

He rubbed his chin and gave her a lopsided grin. "Nothing's broken."

"I wish I'd done something. I *should* have stopped him."

"Nothing you could do," he said. "The governor was saving face. Teaching me a lesson."

"Come over to the bed and lie down."

As he sat heavily on the side of the bed, the fluffy white duvet billowed around him. He pulled her close against his chest and whispered in her ear. "Be careful what you say. I'm sure the room is bugged, and there may be video." He glanced up toward the chandelier. "That's a good place to hide a fish-eye camera."

Worried, she asked, "How's your vision?"

"Fine."

She lightly touched the swelling on his jaw. "Does it hurt?"

"Not much. I knew the punch was coming so I could turn my head and deflect some of the force." He rubbed his midsection. "Didn't expect the gut shot."

"I'll get a washcloth."

The door to the adjoining bathroom stood slightly ajar. Inside, she found a white tiled room with no windows. The fixtures were ornate and gold. She took one of the hand towels, embroidered with a stylized crest showing a sword and a dragon. The crest of St. George? As if the thuglike governor deserved royal attention? Disgusted she dampened the towel with cold water and returned to John.

"Hold this against the bruise," she said as she handed over the cloth. "It's not ice. But the cold might help with the swelling."

Quickly, she explored the room. No phone. No television. Inside the cherry wood armoire, she found a couple of terry-cloth bathrobes. In the drawer under the hanging space, there were packaged slippers.

Still wearing her dress and platform sandals from the cocktail party, she was ready to change into something more comfortable. She found her size in a pair of black ballet slippers and put them on. "Good," she muttered. "Now all I need is a pair of pajamas."

John came up behind her and slid his arms around her. "You really don't think I'm going to let you sleep tonight, do you?"

Was he talking about sex? That wasn't going to happen tonight. No way would she lose her virginity in a gilded prison with guards outside the door and a video camera recording her every move.

She turned in his arms, faced him and studied his expression. His eyes darted toward the chandelier where there might be a fish-eye camera. "Pretend," he whispered.

Though his embrace felt warm and wonderful, she didn't know why they needed to put on a show. She snuggled into the crook of his neck. In a barely audible voice, she said, "What are you thinking?"

"That we need to escape from here. We have to meet Robert."

"No." She pushed away from him. Apparently, John hadn't learned his lesson. But she had. If they did as Ramon ordered, they could leave this island safely.

"Come on, Lily." Again, he glanced toward the suspected hiding place for a camera in the chandelier. "You want this as much as I do."

If anyone was watching, this interaction would look like a lover's quarrel. In her mind, the true meaning was crystal clear. John wanted to escape, to meet up with Robert and rob a bank.

She chose her words carefully. "I'm tired. I just want to sleep."

"We have only one more night in paradise." He held out his hand to her. "Come to the window."

Reluctantly, she placed her hand in his. The warmth of his touch surged through her. Escaping from the mansion was a suicide mission. Not to mention robbing a bank. She'd have to be crazy to agree.

He pushed aside the heavy brocaded drapes and the filmy white sheers. The window overlooked the well-lit cobblestone front driveway where a taxi waited near the entrance. Two guards were posted beside the three-tiered fountain. One of them puffed on a cigarette.

"Look at that moon," John said.

Obediently, she looked skyward. Above the fronds of the palm trees, a round moon looked back at her. She'd always thought a full moon represented good luck.

He unfastened the latch and pushed the window open. "Smell that ocean air. We don't have anything like this back home in Denver."

"Not tonight," she said firmly.

Still, she couldn't help assessing their chance for escape. The window ledge was only fifteen feet off the ground. Directly below them was a landscaped border and a couple of small fat palm trees that would provide cover if they survived the drop without breaking an ankle.

"This is crazy, John."

"Nobody has to know. We came all this way...to be alone."

"Forget it."

She backed away from the window and returned to the room. In the drawer of a bureau, she found clothing. T-shirts with rock-band logos and shorts that looked like they belonged to a teenager. These ought to fit her just fine. She grabbed a black shirt with a Gothic script logo for a band called Iguana Yum-Yum and went into the bathroom to change.

Though she hated giving up on their mission to bring Robert Prescott safely back to Denver, the alternative was too great a risk. Evangeline would understand.

Lily splashed water on her face, washing away the

remnants of her cocktail party makeup. She didn't like to give up. What if Robert attempted to rob the bank by himself? He'd surely be apprehended. And, as Ramon St. George had pointed out, Robert Prescott had many enemies. He wouldn't be offered safe passage back to Denver. If the governor didn't kill him, someone else would.

She thought of Ted Hawley. Somewhere on this island, the Denver cop was probably laughing his butt off. His plan to blow them up in their honeymoon suite had gone awry, but he still had the satisfaction of knowing that he'd thwarted their plans. He'd won.

Could she live with that?

She returned to the bedroom, where John was stretched out on the sheets, still dressed. His eyes were closed, and she hoped he had fallen asleep and forgotten his plan to join Robert. Careful not to disturb him, she lay beside him and pulled the fluffy duvet up to her chin.

His black hair contrasted with the snowy pillow. He'd allowed the drape to close but hadn't turned off the bedside lamps. Soft light shone on his high cheekbones and broad forehead. She'd known him for months, noticed how handsome he was from the first minute she'd walked into Prescott Personal Securities. But she had never really seen who he was. Someone who could be counted on. An honest man.

His eyelids opened. "I like waking up this way," he said. "With you beside me in bed."

She liked it, too. Unable to resist, she leaned down and kissed him.

He reacted immediately. "Ouch."

"Your jaw," she said. "I forgot."

"That's okay. Hurt me some more."

She nuzzled the hollow of his throat, tasting the salty flavor of his flesh. Her arms stretched to reach across his broad chest. She molded her body to his, wishing that their clothes would melt away.

He arranged the duvet so they were both under the covers, hidden from spying cameras. He whispered, "This isn't the way I want to make love to you."

"Me, neither." Losing her virginity shouldn't be like this, even if she wanted him desperately, passionately. Her heart fluttered inside her rib cage like a caged bird aching to be free.

"I'm going to meet Robert," he said. "Can't leave him here. Not after all he's been through."

"I don't see how we can possibly—"

He silenced her by placing his finger across her lips. "You stay here. I'll go alone."

Her passion instantly transformed to anger. "That's not your decision."

"I don't want to put you in more danger."

"I'm your partner, John. We go together. Or not at all."

His dark eyes challenged her. "I'm going."

"So am I."

His plan was simple. They'd toss around under the covers, pretending to have wild sex. Then they'd turn off the light and act like they were asleep. "After an hour," he said, "the surveillance guys will get bored with watching us. We slide off the bed and out the window."

"You're on," she said.

Their fake sex started with John tearing off his shirt. Not to be outdone, she pulled off the Iguana Yum-Yum T-shirt over head. Her lacy beige bra was less revealing than most of the bikini tops she'd seen on the beach.

"Throw off the covers," he whispered. "Give the surveillance boys something to look at."

Straddling his hips, she rose above the covers, threw back her head and writhed dramatically. Feeling as sexy as a porn star, she arched her back and wiggled her shoulders.

"Nice moves," John whispered.

She stretched on top of him. "I never knew sex could be so fun."

"We haven't even gotten to the good part."

He flipped her onto her back and rose above her. Without actually touching her, he bounced up and down as if he was doing push-ups. This wasn't real, but she was definitely getting turned on.

After a few minutes, he whispered, "It's time."

"For what?"

"Your fake orgasm."

Gasping, she called out his name. Synchronizing with his push-ups, she yelled the clichés she'd seen in the movies. "Oh, yes. Baby, you're the best."

His shoulders were shaking, and she realized he was laughing. Stifling her own urge to chuckle, she shouted, "That's right, baby. Oh, yes. Give it to me, big boy."

He collapsed on top of her, and they harmonized in moans of phony ecstasy.

Rolling off her, John turned off the bedside lamp. "Tell me, Lily? Was that good for you?"

"I can honestly say that I've never done anything like that before."

Chapter Eleven

Escaping through the window was easier than John had anticipated. After a long period of stillness under the covers, he and Lily had crawled across the carpeted floor to the long drape. When he peeked through the window and saw no one watching, he'd slipped over the ledge. Lily had followed his lead. As she dropped, he'd caught her in his arms.

The whole maneuver took less than ninety seconds.

Lily gave him a thumb's up. They were both okay. So far, so good.

Now came the hard part: the waiting.

Crouched behind the thick flowering hibiscus, shrubs and palm trees bordering the mansion, he scanned the cobblestone drive. The night was silent except for the splattering of the water in the three-tiered fountain, which would help cover the sounds of their escape.

His adrenaline surged. He wanted to run like hell and hope for the best. But that wasn't his way. He planned. He thought ahead. He survived.

A sound near the mansion's front door attracted his attention. He saw one of the guards step outside and stroll toward the fountain. His easygoing gait gave no indication that he was expecting trouble. A good sign. If the men observing their room had noticed their escape, guards would have been on high alert.

John sat back on his heels to wait for the right moment. Though they had less than an hour until they met with Robert at Pirate's Cove, he needed to be patient. To choose his next move carefully.

A calm settled over him. He remembered his childhood on the reservation when he'd practiced climbing across pine forests and mesas without making a sound. Not the snap of a twig. Nor the rustle of a loose pebble. Not even the hiss of breathing. On hunting trips, his father had taught him the art of silence, blending into the surroundings and waiting for their prey.

On Cuerva, John was the hunted. He and Lily.

A second guard joined the first. The two men talked and lit cigarettes.

John's plan was to circle to the rear of the mansion where the patio overlooked the town and the sea beyond. Earlier today, during the cocktail party, he'd peered over that cliffside terrain, not knowing that he'd need a mental map of the area.

As the guards paced side by side toward the opposite end of the house, he motioned to Lily. She nodded. In the reflected moonlight, her eyes showed no fear. She'd committed one hundred percent to their plan.

Leading the way, he edged around the corner of the mansion. Again, he motioned for her to stop. And they waited. A light shone from an upstairs window. From the patio, he heard the shuffle of footsteps. Someone walking.

To avoid being sighted from the patio, they needed to move away from the shelter of the mansion. He pointed the way, and she followed. Hopping over a stone retaining wall, they were perched at the edge of the steep cliff. Thick bushes and vines crawled up the sides of the limestone rocks. Though it was difficult to gauge distances in the night, John guessed the vertical drop was about forty feet. If he thought too much about the descent, it would be impossible. He turned off his brain and relied on childhood instincts to show him where to place his feet. One step at a time.

There were other sounds in this tropical forest. The hum of insects. The cries of parrots and terns. The rustle of small animals. He lowered himself slowly, finding small footholds between the rocks, clinging to the vines for balance.

Lily slipped. Though he caught her before she fell too far and she didn't cry out, she'd knocked a few rocks loose. The clatter of pebbles sounded as loud as gunshots. He held her close against him and wedged into a narrow crevice. Waiting. Hardly breathing.

From the patio, he heard footsteps. The beam of a flashlight swept across the rocks toward them.

He felt Lily's heart beating against his chest. His plan had put her in danger. If they were caught, he didn't want to think about what might happen to her.

He cared deeply about this small woman. More than he would have thought possible.

She might have been right about accepting the governor's offer and allowing themselves to be deported. He shouldn't have put her in more danger. But he couldn't abandon Robert Prescott, his mentor and friend. Robert had the key to solving the murders in Denver.

John couldn't turn his back and walk away.

The beam of the flashlight came closer. Near their hiding place, a parrot squawked and flew away from the branch of a lemon tree near the patio.

The flashlight passed over them and moved on.

The guard on the patio had not sighted them.

Their descent became more of a slope, and John covered the ground quickly. As they entered a thickly forested area, he took Lily's hand and gave a squeeze. Quietly, he said, "The hard part is over."

"Wish I had better shoes," she muttered. "These ballet slippers aren't great for climbing."

"You did good." He leaned down and kissed her forehead. "Now we go to the hotel and retrieve the stuff we hid under the tiki hut."

She nodded. "I can't wait to have a gun in my hand."

They made their way quickly through the streets, sticking to the back roads. In spite of the explosion, the mood on Cuerva was festive as groups of dancers in blue-footed-booby costumes entertained the tourists and passed out their lucky tokens.

Lily pointed to a shop that was still open. "Do you think we could stop and buy me a pair of decent shoes?"

"It's always about clothes with you."

"These slippers don't have much of a sole. They're already ruined."

"But I like the shorts." The clothes she'd randomly pulled out of a drawer at the mansion didn't fit, but they were tight in all the best places.

"I need the shoes. Otherwise, I'm going to trip over my own feet."

It was easy to be swept away in the party atmosphere, but he didn't lose sight of the facts. If they were spotted by the police, they'd go directly to jail without passing go. Any of the governor's men were a threat. And Hawley was still at large. "We can't risk exposure. And where are you going to buy shoes at this time of night?"

"That makes sense," she said. "Guess I wasn't cut out to be a fugitive."

Avoiding the street lights, they circled the hotel. The space that had once been their honeymoon suite was a gaping, charred maw festooned with yellow crime scene tape. A reminder of how close they'd come to a fiery death.

On the beachfront, the calypso band was playing. And the bar in the tiki hut was doing a brisk business. Sneaking around to the rear and grabbing the objects they'd stashed under the wood floor wouldn't be easy.

"I'll distract the bartenders," Lily said. "You get the stuff."

"Too dangerous." He reminded her, "We're trying not to be noticed."

"Have you got a better plan?"

He thought for a moment. Nothing came to him. "I don't."

Her head swiveled as she scanned the people nearby. "I don't see any police. Or Ted Hawley."

Nor did he. "How will you distract them?"

She fluttered her eyelashes. "My secret."

As she approached the bar at the front of the tiki hut, she tied the T-shirt high on her midriff and rolled up the sleeves to expose as much flesh as possible. She climbed up on a bar stool and danced loosely to the music. The last thing John saw before darting around to the rear was Lily sitting on the bar.

He dug under the wood floor of the hut and retrieved their guns and holsters as well as the bank schematics and the tool kit from Edgar. From the front of the bar, he heard shouts of encouragement and a cheer. Silently, he faded back into the surrounding trees.

In minutes, Lily joined him. Her cheeks were flushed. A silly grin lingered on her lips, and she smelled like rum.

"What did you do?" he asked.

"A bar trick."

"Care to explain?"

"I can drink a shot without using my hands. It's all in the teeth and the tongue. Kind of a handy little skill and harder than it looks. You wouldn't believe how much I had to practice to—"

He motioned for her to be quiet. Someone was approaching. A tall man in a booby costume. He whispered, "It is I. Edgar."

Lily was delighted to see somebody who was on their side. Impulsively, she threw her arms around his feathery middle. "I missed you. You big booby."

"How did you find us?" John asked.

"I caught a glimpse of you in town while dancing with other boobies. Very fortunate, I must say, because I have a message from Robert. And I was delighted by Lily's bar trick."

"Thank you," she said.

"Indeed." He patted her shoulder. "I have only a moment, dear. There is a change in plans. Robert will meet you beside the pirate statue in the square. He is driving a small red vehicle. An ancient Datsun, I think."

"A car?" She was so tired of walking. "Fantastic."

"Go there as soon as possible," Edgar said. "Good luck."

With a flap of his booby wings, he returned to the beachfront festivities.

Her spirits lifted. Maybe it was the shot of rum she'd just guzzled, but Lily felt a burst of optimism. "Did you hear that, John? A car."

"A boat might be more useful." He grinned with half his mouth. The other side of his jaw was swollen. "I'm ready to get the hell off Cuerva."

"I'll second that motion."

Glad that John had memorized a map of the town and local landmarks, she followed his lead. Avoiding the streetlights and traffic, they made their way toward a more residential area. Through the trees on the seaward side of the street, she saw a marina with a forest of tall white masts. Their escape route? Surely, Robert had planned their getaway.

In a small town square, surrounded on three sides by upscale houses, she saw a carved, life-sized statue of a pirate with a cutlass in one hand and a bottle of rum in the other. He was the sentinel for this very classy neighborhood. Lily assumed this was where the bankers and lawyers lived. The professional class. The modern-day pirates.

Several cars were parked at the edge of the park. They zeroed in on a beat-up red Datsun and climbed into the backseat together.

Robert Prescott turned in the front seat and faced them. The streetlamps glistened in his silver hair. He smiled. "Good job."

"With what?" John asked. His tone was irritated. "Being cuffed and arrested? Or being held prisoner by the governor? We don't deserve congratulations for either of those things. Maybe we should get a pat on the back for not getting ourselves blown to bits."

"Quite so," Robert said with a very British stiff upper lip. "I don't suppose you know who planted the bomb?"

"His name is Ted Hawley," Lily said. "I saw him earlier, but it took a while to place him. He's a cop I used to work with in Denver. He must have been hired to get rid of us."

"By Clive Fuentes," Robert said darkly.

"Is he here on the island?"

"Of course not. If he were close, I would know. I'd find him."

His fixation on Clive Fuentes bothered her. The spectrum for possible assailants should also include the governor and Drew Kirshner. With Robert, the focus always came back to his former mentor. She didn't like being sucked into someone else's obsession.

Robert spoke to John. "Did you have a chance to study the bank blueprints?"

"The safest break-in is entry through the duct system on the rooftop."

"Exactly what I thought," Robert confirmed. "I've come prepared with equipment to scale the walls."

"Thoughtful," Lily muttered under her breath.

"Getting past the security system will be difficult," John said. "If I cut all electricity, I'll set off alarms. But I can re-route and disable certain circuits to deactivate a portion of the security system. If I miscalculate, the police will be immediately alerted."

"Then you can't miss," Robert said confidently.

"It's a damn good thing that we don't need to access the money in the vault," John said. "That's where the security is tightest, requiring two thumbprints and special keys. The safe door is virtually impregnable."

"All I need," Robert said, "is access to the main computer system."

She couldn't believe they were really going through with this caper. Breaking into a bank was a gigantic risk, especially when half the people on this island wanted to kill them. "There must be another way. A safer approach."

"None that I can see."

She met Robert's gaze. He didn't look like a crazy man, but his plan was so extreme. "Evangeline wants you home safely. Isn't that more important than your revenge against Clive Fuentes?"

A grimace of pain pulled at the corners of his mouth. "I've put Evangeline through hell. I'm well aware of that."

"You could end it right now," she said. "We can find a way off this island and go back to Denver."

Robert lifted his chin. "John, I'd like to hear your opinion."

John slung his arm around her shoulders. "I agree with Lily. Forget about Clive and bank robberies. Come home with us. Now."

His eyes were haunted. "This isn't entirely about revenge. Clive is the dark presence behind all the prior murders in Denver. His greed. His criminal genius."

"What about the police?" she asked. "Can't we call in the FBI?"

"After two years of searching, I still haven't located Clive. He's changed his identity and could be anywhere in the world." He frowned. "Another reason I can't simply call the authorities is that much of the evidence I've obtained hasn't come through legal channels."

She'd guessed as much. Bank robbery—even in Cuerva—wouldn't look good in a trial.

"This evidence," John said. "Does that include the encrypted list of land coordinates that mysteriously showed up at PPS?"

"It does."

"And you chose to go through us instead of notifying the authorities."

"A measured and logical decision," Robert said. "Cassie Allen is brilliant at deciphering codes. I trusted that Evangeline would make the proper decisions. Just as I know this bank robbery is necessary. Not only will we flush out Clive by cutting off his money supply, but we will obtain the list of investors in Kingston Trust. The final clue that will lead toward a final solution."

Despite her exhaustion and her common sense, Lily felt herself being swayed toward Robert's plan. His rationale for ending the string of murders made sense. She knew how tedious the legal system could be.

"We're running out of time," Robert said. "I can't wait for the slow turning of the wheels of justice. I need to protect my family. When I heard about the attack on Peter Turner, I knew Clive was getting too close. No one will be safe until he's apprehended."

The desperation in his voice touched her. Robert's intentions were good. He wanted to protect his family.

"I won't force you," he said quietly. "I realize that I'm asking you both to risk your lives. A request I don't take lightly. I'll leave you alone for five minutes to make your decision."

He slipped out of the car and closed the door.

She sank back in the seat and leaned against John's chest. "What are our chances of getting in and out of the bank without being discovered?"

"Assuming that we actually get inside the building, I'd say the odds are slightly in our favor. Sixty-forty."

She'd wanted to hear something in the neighbor-hood of ninety percent. "I thought you were an expert in security systems."

"Not when I'm working without the benefit of state-of-the-art computerized and electronic equipment. If I had the right tools, I could guarantee that we'd get past the system. Even then, one of the night watchmen might see us."

She looked up at him. Shadows outlined his strong features. That was the right word for John. *Strong.* Also, *capable.*

She wouldn't trust her fate to Robert. Or even to Edgar. But if John wanted to go forward with this plan, she'd do it. "What do you think? Should we rob this bank?"

"Logically, I'm not convinced that there isn't another way to access this computer information. There's no such thing as a completely secure firewall protection. Not for any computer."

She thought of Lenny. The resident computer expert at PPS had been the most lovable geek she'd ever known. He had been killed in an explosion. Other people had died. Peter Turner was in a coma, clinging to life by a thread. The danger was real. The threat couldn't be ignored.

"This decision isn't about logic," she said. "It's about protecting the people we care about."

His lips brushed her forehead. "I care about you."

As much as Robert cared about Evangeline? And his son? "We can't say no. If Robert's plan will end this threat to PPS, we have to do it."

His head dipped lower and he lightly kissed her lips. "I knew you'd say that."

"How?"

"You're a sucker for a sob story, and you believe in happy endings."

If she were to ever have a happy ending of her own with John, they had to get this right. No mistakes. No missteps. "Let's go rob a bank."

Chapter Twelve

As they drove through the streets, Lily began seeing Cuerva as a patchwork of tourism and high finance. On the main street and beachfront, calypso bands serenaded the festival of the blue-footed booby. It was a carnival atmosphere, filled with brilliant color and laughter.

In the financial district, the streets were devoid of traffic. The buildings were solid and somber. The Bank St. George—a heavy, three-story structure of rough-hewn stone blocks—occupied a corner where one of the few stoplights in town blinked red, amber and green.

Robert parked a few blocks away and killed the headlights. When they stepped into the night, the silence was profound, almost reverent.

From the trunk of the rusted Datsun, Robert produced ropes and a grappling hook. John used his money belt and his pockets to carry the equipment Edgar had provided. All Lily had was the automatic pistol strapped in a holster to her bare leg.

She whispered, "What's my part? What am I supposed to do?"

"You're the lookout," John said.

Robert added, "If necessary, you need to neutralize the two night watchmen."

If "neutralize" meant murder, she was in trouble. Though she wouldn't hesitate to use her gun to threaten, she couldn't bring herself to kill innocent bank guards. There was a better way. She'd rely on her extensive martial arts training—skills she'd honed when she was a cop.

With justifiable pride, she remembered ending a fight in a motorcycle bar. With a couple of well-placed kicks and leverage holds, she'd subdued the troublemakers and taken them into custody. After that incident, she'd been tagged with the reputation of looking like Tinkerbelle but striking like a Mack truck. That rep was one of the reasons Ted Hawley had made a move against her...and ended up flat on his butt.

Lily was confident that she could "neutralize" the night watchmen without causing them permanent damage.

She followed Robert and John into the alley behind the bank. Standing clear, she watched as Robert threw the grappling hook over the top ledge. The clatter of steel against stone echoed in the deserted alley. The hook caught. Robert pulled the rope taut and started climbing the wall. John went next.

As soon as he reached the top, she started up. In spite of the gloves Robert had provided, the rope bit into her hands. Her flimsy ballet slippers offered very little traction, but she scampered up the wall like a spider whose web was on fire. John hauled her over the edge and pulled the rope up behind her.

From the top of the building, she could see the lights from the hotels and the festival and the marina. A Caribbean breeze freshened her cheeks, and a shiver of excitement went through her. She'd heard that criminals got a rush from their illegal acts. That must be what she was feeling. A giddy thrill.

Robert had already unfastened the screws on an air vent and pried off the cover. He shone a flashlight into the round metallic shaft, and Lily peered inside. As far as she could tell, it went straight down, then turned at a right angle. The dimensions were narrow. Extremely narrow. A tight fit, even for her.

"I was afraid of this," John said. "The blueprints were unclear about the size of the shaft."

She looked toward a small square building on the rooftop that must have been the regular access. "Can't we just go through that door?"

John shook his head. "If that door is opened from this side, an alarm sounds."

"And if it's opened from the inside?" she asked.

"No problem."

She returned to the shaft and stared down. "I can fit."

"Right," Robert said briskly. "This metal tube goes straight down five feet then hooks up with another ventilation tube. The hardest part will be making that ninety degree turn. Go to the right. In about twenty yards you'll reach the elevator shaft.

There are several ladders. Climb to one of the doorways that open onto the stairwell. Come back up top and open the door for us."

He had the solution so quickly that she wondered if he'd known from the start that he'd need somebody small to crawl through the ductwork. "Did you ask for me on this assignment because I'm short?"

"Evangeline assigned you," Robert said. "She suspected I might need your skill in martial arts. And she thought you would balance John's somewhat stoic personality."

"She thinks I'm a party girl?"

"Does the shoe fit?"

His light teasing—especially in the midst of a bank robbery—held a certain charm. A rakish grin contrasted the silver in his hair. She was beginning to understand why Evangeline was so in love with her husband that she'd never given up faith in his return. Even after two years. Even after being told that he was dead.

When John turned her toward him, she wondered if the attraction she felt toward him could become something as deep and fulfilling as the love of Robert and Evangeline.

He frowned, obviously concerned. "I don't like this plan, Lily."

"Neither do I, but it can't be helped."

With exquisite tenderness, he stroked her cheek and the line of her jaw. They'd been through so much in such a short time. These had been the most intense days of her life.

He said, "If you don't want to do this, I'll understand."

"I'll give it a try."

She met his gaze. An unspoken communication flowed between them. They had memories. They'd shared secrets and trusts. She didn't want to let him down.

"Well, well," Robert said. "It seems that Evangeline made the correct choice in putting you together."

"Right." She echoed his brisk tone as she leaned down to remove the holster from her leg. She needed to be as sleek as possible to fit through the duct. "I need to go head first. You guys will have to hold my feet."

With her hands over her head like a diver, she entered the tube. In her mouth, she held a penlight—the only illumination in this dark, narrow space that was barely wide enough for her shoulders. At the intersection of the tubes, she braced herself in a handstand. She needed to go right and pointed her hands in that direction.

As John lowered her slowly by her feet, she wedged around the sharp turn until she was lying flat on her back with her arms over her head. Though she wasn't claustrophobic, this tight squeeze was scary as hell. What if she got stuck? She could be trapped in this pipe forever.

Using her feet and hips, she inched forward. Twenty yards? It seemed like twenty miles.

Craning her neck, she shone the light toward her hands. Nothing but darkness. What if Robert was wrong about the direction?

Though air moved inside the duct, her lungs clenched. It was hard to breathe, but she had an urge to scream. She kept moving, inch by painful inch. Her eyelids closed tightly. And she thought of John. His eyes. His lips. At the end of this tunnel, she'd find him. They'd be together. She had to make that happen.

Her outstretched hands felt open space. The elevator shaft. Cautiously, she pushed herself forward until her arms and head were in the shaft. She took the penlight in her hand and searched. The rungs of a metal ladder were less than a foot away.

Clinging with both hands, she maneuvered her way out of the duct and swung free, supporting herself with her arms. When her toes rested on another rung of the ladder, she gulped down air. There was the stink of heavy machinery. Oil and grit.

She'd gone from being compressed in a tube to dangling on a ladder inside an elevator shaft. Not a great trade-off. At least she could breathe.

Climbing up, she found a door beside the ladder, shoved it open and stepped into a stairwell. Though the night watchmen patrolled at irregular intervals, she felt safe as she skipped up the stairs to the top floor and opened the door.

John came through first. He gathered her into his embrace. "You had me scared. What took you so long?"

"I was purposely dawdling because I enjoy being jammed inside a metal toothpaste tube."

He gave her a quick hard kiss. "Never do that again."

"Don't worry. This won't be a regular habit."

Robert cleared his throat. "We should hurry."

Now that they were inside the bank, they needed to move fast. Lily slipped on a pair of thin latex gloves to avoid leaving fingerprints. "Do you think there will be an investigation?"

"I doubt you'll need to worry about being extradited back to Cuerva," Robert said. "The activities of Kingston Trust are clearly illegal and the governor will want this connection to be hushed up."

"Like the explosion he called an accident."

"Precisely."

They took the stairwell all the way down to the basement level where John popped open a metal box filled with complicated-looking circuitry.

As he consulted the schematic, snipped various wires and tied off others, she had absolutely no idea what he was doing. But she believed in him. He wouldn't make a mistake.

Returning to the stairwell, they went to the first floor. Slowly, John opened the door and eased through. She and Robert followed. To their right was the main lobby with marble floors, vaulted ceilings and a row of teller cages in front of the walk-in vault. The lofty decor reminded her of a pagan cathedral dedicated to the worship of the offshore banking gods.

To their left was a more humble office area with a waiting area and receptionist's desk in the center. Offices behind glass walls ranged on either side. Across the wood-paneled back wall were two closed doors. She assumed those offices belonged to the important bank officials and were their destination.

John put on a pair of weird goggles with telescoping lenses that had been in the package Edgar had slipped into her purse. He frowned as he took them off and handed them to her.

When she looked through, the light-sensitive alarm system became visible. Several threads of red light criss-crossed the lobby and the office area.

John whispered, "Tell me when the lights are off."

He knelt and used a special instrument to open a small metal panel near the baseboard. After a few minutes, the red lights snapped off.

"Now," she said.

Before they moved forward, John reached up and disconnected the feed on a rotating camera.

They crept forward. Instead of approaching the rear offices, they entered the glass cubicle nearest the receptionist's desk.

Robert took the seat behind the computer screen. He flicked the switch. Nothing happened. He tried it again. "Something's wrong."

She heard the clunk of rubber-soled shoes on the marble floor of the main lobby. The night watchman.

She could handle him. Giving a signal to John and Robert, she edged silently toward the lobby. Hiding at the edge of the teller's cages, she waited. Her breathing was steady, and her mind was calm as she visualized the necessary moves to disable the watchman using the pressure points at his wrist, elbow and throat.

She measured his forward progress by the sound of his footfalls. His sneakers squeaked on the marble floor. His pace was leisurely. He seemed to be stopping frequently to look around.

A static buzz from his walkie-talkie echoed against the high ceilings.

His voice was low and gruff. "Which camera is on the fritz?"

The static voice answered.

"In the front office? Okay. I'll check."

He came even with her. Lily moved swiftly. A kick. A twist of his arm. Pressure against the nerve center in his throat. He went down with a thud. Out cold. Neutralized.

When she turned toward the rear office area, she saw John coming toward her. "This is more complicated than I thought," he said. "We need to circumvent the internal wiring and reactivate the—"

"Bottom line," she said. There wasn't time for him to give her a tutorial on how security systems worked.

"We need to take out the other guard."

"And then?" she asked.

"We have seven minutes before the silent alarm alerts the police to a break-in."

She gave a quick nod. "I'll take care of the watchman. You do whatever it is you need to do."

They approached the security office near the front entrance. The second watchman sat in front of a bank of screens—live feeds from the various cameras.

Before he could react, Lily found his pressure point. Within seconds, he was unconscious.

"Cool," John said. "How'd you do that?"

"Aikido pressure points. I like to call it the Vulcan Death Grip, but nobody dies. Let's move."

He flipped a series of switches. "That should do it."

They returned to the rear area where Robert was already working on the computer.

"Five and a half minutes," John warned him.

Without speaking, Robert focused intently on the keyboard. A series of numbers cascaded across the screen. She read the words "Kingston Trust" at the top of the page. In a few keystrokes, Robert raised his hands.

"It's done," he said. "Every penny of the Kingston Trust funds have been transferred to my own coded Swiss account. That should force Clive out of hiding."

"Three minutes," John said.

"Now I need the list of investors."

Robert bent over the keyboard again. A message flashed on the screen. "Access denied."

"Damn. I need one more password. It's six letters."

"One minute," John said. "We have to go."

"Can't leave without this. Six letters. Not Kingston. Something with TCM. Maybe Denver." He tried it. "Access denied."

"Try Turner," John said. TCM was run by Stephen and Olivia Turner.

"Access denied."

The answer popped inside Lily's brain. When Olivia and Stephen's son Peter had awakened from his coma, he spoke one word. "Coyote," she said. "Try it."

The file opened.

TED HAWLEY DISCONNECTED THE call, snapped his cell phone closed and tossed it on the car seat beside him. His employer had reprimanded him, treated him like a kid who hadn't done his done his homework.

Damn Lily Clark. This was her fault. Even when he packed her room with C-4 explosive, the little bitch refused to die.

According to Ted's employer, Lily was at Bank St. George. She and her boyfriend had pulled off some kind of computerized heist that had triggered an alarm halfway around the world.

It was Ted's job to stop them. His real target was Robert Prescott, who had to be taken alive.

Lily and her boyfriend were expendable.

Ted turned the key in the ignition. He shouldn't have trusted the governor to keep her locked up, should have known that she'd find her way free.

"Not for long," he muttered as he drove toward the Cuerva financial district. This time, he wouldn't leave anything to chance. He would watch her take her last breath.

Chapter Thirteen

Inside the bank, the minutes ticked down to zero. Then one minute beyond. Two minutes.

Every muscle in John's body clenched. He knew the police had been alerted to the robbery in progress. At any second, they could be here.

Hurry, Robert. Damn it, hurry.

The computer clicked and hummed, downloading the information they needed. Not fast enough.

John glanced toward Lily who stood between the office area and the front lobby, checking to make sure neither of the watchmen woke up. She was poised to take off. Her gun was in hand.

"Done." Robert pulled the zip drive from the computer. "I've got the list of investors."

"Let's go."

There wasn't time to make a fancy exit from the rooftop. The cops were on their way. They had to run.

As they sprinted through the lobby, he heard groans from the first watchman Lily had disabled. Couldn't worry about him. Had to move fast.

They burst through the front door of the bank. As soon as it opened, a shrill alarm sounded. But the streets were still deserted. The cops hadn't yet responded. Not surprising. From what John had seen, the Cuerva police weren't exactly a crack law enforcement team.

Robert led the way, racing around the corner of the Bank St. George toward the beat-up red Datsun.

The alarm continued to scream.

They piled into the car, and Robert pulled away from the curb. "We're going to the docks," he said. "It will be necessary to separate. Meet at the boat named *Martina*."

John recalled the name on the Cessna that had been sabotaged on their way to Cuerva. "Edgar's boat."

"He remains fixated on that woman. His one true love. Martina."

A few blocks away from the bank, John heard approaching police sirens—a reminder that they still weren't out of danger.

A dull pain unfurled inside his head, behind his eyes. Ever since he'd lowered Lily into that metal duct and watched her disappear into darkness, his stress level had been high…too high. The headache hammered steadily, beating in time with his pulse. The edges of his vision blurred. The tension had caught up to him. He was going blind.

"John." Lily tugged at his shirt sleeve. "Look at me."

He shook his head. If he couldn't see well enough

to escape, that was his own damn problem. She shouldn't have to pay for his disability. "I'm fine," he murmured.

"Look at me."

He turned his head toward her. Her face was a pale blur, sinking into a thick darkness.

"My eyes," she said. "Concentrate on my eyes."

Though he'd never been able to control these bouts of temporary blindness, he tried to do as she said. *Focus.* The pain inside his skull narrowed to a piercing needle. He squeezed his eyelids shut, then opened them. The darkness lifted. Not much. Only a flicker.

But he could see the shape of her eyes. Beautiful, glowing eyes. A rich whisky-brown.

Fighting the darkness, he stared. Her features seemed more clear, but he wasn't sure if that was true or if he was imagining it.

The car jolted, and Lily bounced against him. He saw her grin. The light returned. He was going to be all right. "We're going to make it," he said.

Robert parked the car in a lot outside the marina. "I'll go through the gate," he said. "You two climb the fence and meet me at the *Martina.*"

"Why?" Lily asked.

"The night watchman will ask for proper authorization. Which you don't have."

She exhaled an exasperated sigh. "How about if we all go together and I neutralize the watchman if he gives us any trouble."

"Much as I appreciate your martial arts skill,"

Robert said, "I prefer not to leave a string of unconscious victims in our wake."

"I wouldn't really hurt him."

"But the police might question him, and I don't want to give an indication of our escape route."

She nodded. "Agreed. We'll follow your lead."

While Robert marched up to the gate, John and Lily ran along the edge of a six-foot-high chain-link fence—a flimsy barrier to protect the marina. Using a clump of palm trees for cover, they easily climbed over the fence and crouched in the sand.

Though his head still throbbed, John's vision was okay. He could see Robert's silhouette moving along the dock where the boats were moored.

He glanced down at Lily. In the moonlight, her features were clear. Her lips parted in a slow, sexy grin. "In just a few minutes," she said, "we're going to be off this damn island."

"Going home."

"It's funny, but I never really think of Denver as home."

"Where then?"

"Whenever anyone asks, I always say I'm from Ann Arbor. That's where my parents live."

Home was the place where you connected to the land, where you had roots and family. "I want you to come to my home. Meet my parents and my sister."

"Wait a minute." She gave him a startled look. "Are you telling me that you still live with your mom and dad?"

"Not in the same house." He kept an eye on Robert's progress toward the end of the dock. "Nearby."

"I'd like to meet them." As she spoke, Lily realized that she actually would like to know his family. She wanted to know everything she could about John. "The whole Pinto family tree. Do you call yourselves a tribe?"

"The Navajo nation is the tribe. We're part of a clan. The Two Trees clan." He nodded toward the docks. "You go first. Stay low. I'll follow."

She needed no further encouragement. Doubled over, she hurried across the sand toward the dock where Robert had been walking. She'd never been more ready to move on. Her lack of passport was going to present problems. At least she still had her driver's license. Thank God, she'd gotten her purse back from the cops and had insisted that John carry her license in his wallet.

Though she could see the night watchman doing something with ropes near the entrance from the parking lot, she sensed another presence as she stepped onto the floating dock. Hesitating, she listened to the lapping of the water against the hulls of boats and the creaking of the wood slats beneath her feet.

There were probably a hundred small craft— ranging from delicate sailboats to a seventy-foot party boat with a flat hull and a purple canopy. She ducked behind a small shack where orange lifejackets hung in neat rows. Three-quarters of the way down the dock, she saw Robert waiting in a sleek motorboat.

Escape was so close. All she had to do was reach out and grab the brass ring. She could win this prize.

But something wasn't right. Her senses prickled. She could feel danger. Glancing over her shoulder, she saw John coming toward her.

Her gaze lifted. She scanned the chain-link fence. Then she saw him. From this distance, she couldn't identify Ted Hawley, but she knew it was him. He held a gun.

She hit the wood planks of the dock. Simultaneously, she called out. "John, get down."

He did as she said. Without question.

Shots rang out. A bullet splintered into the wood shed behind her.

John flipped to his back. Drew his gun from the ankle holster. From an off-balance position, he fired.

Hawley ducked behind a palm tree.

Her own gun was in her hand. She aimed at the tree and fired three times in rapid succession.

John raced up beside her. Taking turns, they kept up a steady barrage as they moved down the dock.

She heard Hawley yell, "This isn't over, Lily. I know where you live."

Bastard.

She jumped into the boat beside John. Robert expertly steered them through the other moored boats and out of the marina to the open sea. Unless Hawley had a bazooka in his pocket, they were out of range.

At the helm, Robert expertly guided the *Martina* through open waters as he talked into a radio.

Though she didn't know where they were headed, she trusted him.

Beside her, John holstered his gun. "Not exactly a subtle, quiet escape."

"You know how it is with a party girl like me," she said. "I like to go out with a bang."

"Don't get too relaxed," he warned. "The governor could notify authorities on the other islands. We could still be tracked down by helicopters or search planes."

It was so typical of John to think of all the possible disasters and then to make contingency plans. "Not to mention shark attacks," she teased.

"Or tidal waves." He grinned. "Or lightning. And we could run into a hurricane."

"I get it," she said. "We're not safe yet."

Robert aimed their small boat toward a long, palatial yacht—an absolutely gorgeous craft. He waved at the crewmen standing at the railing. A wealthy friend? One of his MI6 contacts?

She looked back at the curved shoreline glistening in the moonlight. They hadn't spent much actual time on Cuerva, but it was enough to be threatened, imprisoned and to rob a bank. Not to mention the special bond that had developed between her and John. And his promise to teach her the secrets of lovemaking.

These few hours on Cuerva had changed her life.

JOHN HAD NEVER BEEN HAPPIER to see the sun setting behind the Rocky Mountain west of Denver. No palm trees. No turquoise Caribbean waves. No long-tailed iguanas. It was good to be home again.

The fresh, dry air swept through the open window of the rental car they'd picked up at a private airport near Boulder. He glanced into the rearview mirror to see Robert, sitting quietly in the backseat. "What do you think, Robert? Is Colorado the way you remembered it?"

"The most beautiful place on earth." His voice was weary. "I'm glad to be back."

John turned to Lily, who sat beside him in the passenger seat. Though he'd thoroughly appreciated the skimpy clothes she'd worn on the island, she looked just as sexy in jeans and a pastel-green T-shirt with a V-neck that showed a hint of cleavage. Behind her dark glasses, he knew her eyes were smiling.

"Does this feel like home?" he asked.

"Finally. I thought we'd never get here."

Their return from Cuerva had taken three days of complicated maneuvering designed to throw off anyone who would be searching for Robert Prescott, and a fancy bit of diplomacy to get Lily past customs without her passport.

The hardest part had been the constant state of alert. Their primary mode of transportation had been private planes and one brief hop on a chopper. They couldn't risk taking a commercial flight with a passenger list that could be traced. Setting a false trail, they'd checked into a hotel room in Manhattan, then left without staying in the room. They'd ridden in cabs, limos and private cars. Throughout this sojourn, he and Lily hadn't been able to let their guard down for a minute. Their only sleep had been catnaps with one eye open.

According to Robert's contacts, the computer transfer of the millions of dollars in the Kingston Trust to his own Swiss account had been successful. He had thrown Clive Fuentes' network of high finance criminals into a state of panic.

The only way they could get their money back was to learn Robert's nine-digit code. The response he had leaked in a direct phone call to Governor Ramon St. George was simple but effective: "If any of my friends or family are harmed, I will donate the money to an International Relief Fund and it will be gone forever."

The only way the bad guys could win was through Robert. He was their target. It had been up to John and Lily to protect him.

She shrugged. "I guess it won't really feel like this is over until I walk through the door to my apartment, water my plants and collapse into my own bed."

"About that." He and Robert had discussed housing arrangements at length. "You need to stay with me until things calm down."

"Why? I live on the seventh floor of a secure high-rise. It's safe."

"Like the honeymoon suite on Cuerva." The memory of that gaping, burned-out maw flashed through his mind. "You remember Ted Hawley's last words to you?"

"I know where you live."

The threat wasn't over. "Hawley might be only a henchman, but he's dangerous."

"I know," she said. "Especially now that I've identified him. And we really need to talk to Mike Lawson, the guy who hooked up with Cassie Allen a couple of months ago."

"Why?"

"Mike's a cop. He'll make sure that Hawley is investigated and gets what's coming to him." A frown pinched her forehead. "I hate to think of Hawley going back to work at the Denver PD. If we can tie him to the bomb at Cassie Allen's place and the Molotov cocktail that killed Lenny, he'll go to jail where he belongs. And he'll probably blame me."

"Undoubtedly."

"You know he's a psycho, right?"

"Which is exactly why you're staying with me. I have decent security at my place. Plus, there are two of us to keep watch."

She shifted in her seat. "How is your mother going to feel when you bring me home?"

"She'll be pleased." More than pleased. She'd be delighted. His mother, Yvonne, wanted him to get married, settle down and give her a dozen grandbabies.

"Since I don't really have much choice in the matter," Lily said, "I accept your invitation. But there is a big, fat problem."

"What's that?"

"I don't have any clothes."

He rolled his eyes. "You and your wardrobe."

"Or shoes." She looked down at the sneakers on

her feet. "I have the perfect climbing boots in my closet at my apartment. And comfortable running shoes. And these really great little sandals with a kitten heel."

Bemused, he listened as she chatted about her shoe collection. The woman was preoccupied with footwear. "We'll buy you some shoes," he promised.

"Spoken like a man. Finding the right shoe takes effort. It's like stalking a wild iguana. Or going on a treasure hunt without a map."

He took a left onto an unmarked two-lane road leading into a canyon.

"Speaking of maps," she said, "where are we going?"

"The PPS safe house. Jack Sanders should be there waiting for us."

"How does he know we're coming?"

John had avoided regular contact with the office, even on supposedly secure phone lines. No traceable connections. "Jack went there to wait as soon as we left Cuerva."

"And the safe house is obviously a secret."

"One hundred percent secure. There are hidden cameras, silent alarms, motion detectors. You name it."

Again, he checked Robert's reflection in the rearview mirror. His old friend stared morosely through the side window. John had expected more excitement. Robert's two-year absence was almost over. Soon, he'd be able to resume his life. Why the gloom?

They passed a rustic general store, a post office and

a couple of quiet little cabins before turning into an area that was marked as National Forest. The final approach to the safe house was a graded gravel road, nearly hidden by the surrounding forest of pines and aspen.

John parked and quickly stepped out.

Two PPS agents—Jack Sanders and Ethan Moore—stood on the porch. They lowered their rifles and called out a greeting.

"Back from the islands," said Jack Sanders. "Real tough assignment, John."

"Don't even start."

He gave Lily a friendly pat on the shoulder. "Nice job, rookie. It's good to have you back safely. Both of you."

After warm greetings with Robert, Sanders led them into the house. John pulled him aside for an update. Both men were former military and spoke the same language. "We got the list of investor names."

Sanders gave a quick nod. He'd been in at the start of these murders when the movie star had been killed. "Is Nick Warner on it?"

"Don't know," John said. "It's a computer file that needs decryption."

"Is Robert going to call in Cassie Allen to handle it? She's the expert."

"Not yet." John watched with concern as Robert followed Ethan toward an office. "Robert wants to do this himself. He's been operating alone for two years. Now that he's so close to the end, the stress has caught up to him."

"You think he might crack?"

"Keep a close eye on him. Don't let him get into trouble."

"Sure thing," Sanders said. "As if anybody can tell Robert Prescott what to do."

Robert was the boss, the founder of PPS. But he wasn't operating at full capacity.

Leaving the others behind, John went into the safe house office where Robert sat behind a computer. He'd already plugged in the zip drive containing the downloaded information from Bank St. George and was staring at the screen with bleary eyes.

John stepped up beside him. "Want to tell me what's bothering you?"

"This list of investor names. It's encrypted and will take some serious efforts to decipher. You know something about codes, don't you?"

John's great-uncle had been one of the Navajo code-talkers in World War II, translating messages from English to his native language, which was indecipherable to the enemy. But John wasn't about to be sidetracked into a discussion of Navajo history. "Don't change the subject, Robert."

"Nothing to talk about. I'm fine."

"You should call in Cassie Allen to do this work."

"If I don't get it figured out by tomorrow, I will. Right now, I want something to work on. To keep myself busy."

Instead of using an expert? That didn't make sense. John closed the door and returned to the desk. "What's the real problem?"

"Evangeline," he said quietly. "I've been away from her for two years. Even worse, I allowed her to believe that I was dead."

"You're back now. You can pick up where you left off."

"I'm not so sure." With a fingertip, he traced a circle on the desktop. "How can I expect her to forgive me?"

The easy answer was that Evangeline was his wife and she adored him. Never once had John heard her say a negative word about her husband. "She loves you."

"I put her through hell, allowed her to mourn my death."

"We had a very nice memorial service," John said. "A decent crowd showed up."

He groaned. "This isn't the sort of thing that I can patch up with a dozen roses and a box of candy."

"You will have to do a hell of a lot better than that," John agreed. "You and Evangeline are going to have to learn to love each other again. Start over."

"Are you suggesting a courtship? With gifts and fine dinners and dating?"

"The whole damn thing."

"A fine idea." He brightened. "Considering that you're still a bachelor, you're rather wise in the ways of women."

"I know about family. When all is said and done, the only thing that really matters is family, especially the love between a husband and wife."

"Perhaps," Robert said, raising an eyebrow, "you'll soon join the ranks of married men. With Lily."

He had already foreseen the potential of a lifetime with Lily at his side. Even though she didn't yet know it, she was his future wife.

Chapter Fourteen

Leaving the PPS safe house, Lily gazed through the windshield at the gathering darkness. Though it was July and still warm after sunset, she shivered. Going home with John made her happy, jittery and a bit terrified. All at the same time.

The happiness came from looking forward to a full night's sleep without the constant tension of being pursued. Of course, there was more than the simple creature comfort of sleep that was making her smile inside. Being with John pleased her. The sound of his voice made her want to sing dopey love songs. And sometimes when she looked at him, she was overwhelmed by a strange and joyful warmth.

And the jitters? Well, who wouldn't be nervous? She couldn't go back to her own apartment because she was a target for Ted Hawley. That creep might still track her down.

What about the terror—the burning terror that clenched her lungs and sent her heart flapping like the wings of a blue-footed booby? John had promised to make love to her. He'd spoken of slow kisses and skilled caresses that would unleash pleasures she'd never felt before.

Tonight might be the time when she lost her virginity. She hadn't planned her life this way. Most people—like Robert Prescott—assumed she was a carefree party girl who wasn't afraid of anything. *So wrong.*

She was terrified of making a fool of herself. Possibly even more frightening was the possibility that John had changed his mind. What if he didn't want her anymore?

The actual distance between his home and the PPS safe house wasn't far on a map, but he estimated that driving out of one canyon, down the road past Golden to another turn-off would take over thirty minutes.

"You're quiet," he said.

"Looking forward to a good night's sleep."

"You've got that right. Feels like we've been up for three days."

But did he want to do more than sleep? In the glow from the dashboard, she couldn't read his expression. For now, it was best to stick to business. "Ethan told me what's been going on around here. Drew Kirshner is back in Denver. He came to the PPS offices, threw a hissy fit and demanded to see you and me."

"Did he say why?"

"Something about how we'd cost him hundreds of thousands of dollars." No doubt, Kirshner had been hurt by the money transfer from the Kingston Trust. "Do you think Kirshner is the one who hired Ted Hawley?".

"Hard to say."

"Come on, John. I know you have an opinion. Give me some of that logic you're so famous for."

He made a left turn into the foothills. Though there were occasional lights along this road, the forest closed around them in a dark embrace.

"Here's how I see it," he said. "Investors in Kingston Trust have been getting killed off one after another. The fact that Kirshner is still alive makes him suspicious. With his connections to the Russian mob, he might be high up the food chain—close to Clive Fuentes."

Given the lack of tangible evidence like checks written to Hawley or phone records, John had pinpointed the most damaging fact: Kirshner was still alive. "Makes sense," she said.

"Also, he was in Cuerva. Close to the money. And Kirshner is a known associate of Governor St. George."

"Because Kirshner lives in Denver," she added, "it's logical that he'd hire a local thug. I can't imagine the mysterious Clive Fuentes having any contact with a jerk like Hawley."

"When I talk to Evangeline," John said, "I'll be sure to mention that we should maintain surveillance on Kirshner."

Surveillance and stakeouts were the kind of jobs most often given to Lily. She expected that to change. After her performance on Cuerva, she rated more high-level assignments. She wasn't an untried rookie anymore. "When do we go back to work?"

"After an assignment like this, Evangeline usually suggests a week off."

"What if I don't want to take time off?"

He took his eyes off the twisty road and looked at her. "You enjoy this, don't you? The intensity. The risk."

"I like it," she admitted.

"Why?"

"The challenge. It sounds like bragging to say this, but it's just genetics. I was a gifted kid. Things always came easily to me. All my life, I've always been looking for ways to test myself. This is it."

They drove for a moment in silence before he said, "Be careful what you ask for, Lily."

He turned right on a graded gravel road into a wide meadow bordered by forested foothills. Nestled amid a stand of round-leaf aspen trees was a long, low, adobe-style house with a sloping tile roof. Lights shone through several windows. Behind the house, she saw the looming shadow of a barn.

"That's where my parents and my sister live," John said. "Over here is my place."

He parked the rental car in front of another adobe structure—two-story with a long balcony running all the way across the second floor and a covered porch beneath it.

When they stepped out of the car, a motion-sensitive light came on, giving her a clear view of his house. The clean lines and wide, square windows made the earth-colored adobe look modern. But the dark wood railing across the balcony and porch was etched with stylized suns, and the front door was carved with primitive etchings. Like John, his house was both state-of-the-art and traditional.

She glanced toward an outbuilding under construction at the side of the house. "Adding on?"

"My own barn," he said. "My parents have horses and goats. I was thinking about getting my own livestock."

"With your schedule? You'd never have time to take care of them."

"There's plenty of help nearby." He pointed to the lights of another distant house. "The Tsotse family lives over there. Four kids. Farther down the road is another retired couple, Jason Iron Deer and his wife."

"All Navajo?"

"When I first moved here, I got a great deal on thirty acres. First my parents came here and built. Then the others."

"But it's still your land."

"No one can really own the earth. We come from the land. She sustains us."

"Not a real popular concept among Realtors."

He went around to the trunk and took out the duffel bag that held the few belongings they'd picked up on the way across the country. "To be honest, I'm not sure how my family ended up moving here. I didn't plan for this to happen, but I'm glad things turned out the way they did. We're settled now."

When he unlocked the front door, he immediately

went to a keypad beside the door and punched in a code to deactivate the alarm. "Opening any door or window on the house sets off a screeching alarm that rings through to the local sheriff's office. More important, it lets my friends and family know I'm in trouble. Within five minutes, they're here."

"Has the alarm ever gone off before?"

"A couple of times by accident. It takes about five minutes for everybody to respond. With guns. They're a tough bunch." He set the duffel bag on a long wooden table. "Mostly, the alarm system is for when I'm not here. Protection against burglary."

As she checked out the interior of his house, she understood why he might be robbed. The walls were hung with Native American lithographs and paintings that picked up the earth tones of the furniture. A clean-line modern sofa in brown leather sat on a beautiful woven rug. Beside it was a heavy Spanish-style chair with thick, carved arms and legs. She zeroed in on a small painting that hung near the adobe fireplace in the corner of the room. "Is this an original?"

"Georgia O'Keefe," he said. "I bought it from a cousin who worked at her ranch in New Mexico."

"Shouldn't this be locked up in a safe?"

"Then no one would appreciate it. Art is meant to be shared."

She nodded. "You're just full of pithy bits of wisdom tonight."

"I'm comfortable now," he said. "I'm home."

Shelves displayed an array of Native American pottery and patterned woven baskets. She stated her earlier opinion. "Modern but traditional. I guess that's a good description of you."

"And there's one tradition we need to follow right now before we get comfortable. When I come home from an assignment I pay a visit to my mother. If we don't stop by to see her, she'll be over here with a pot of stew."

Lily thought of her own parents, whom she spoke to only every other week. Not that they had a bad relationship. They were…distant. They'd raised her to be independent, and she was grateful for that gift. Still, it might have been nice to know that they worried about her occasionally.

When they left his house, John re-activated the alarm. She noticed that he was still wearing his ankle holster. "Should I be armed?" she asked.

"My mother is a hugger, but you probably don't want to shoot her."

"You've got your gun."

John didn't expect trouble, but it never hurt to be prepared. Drew Kirshner had been looking for him and Lily; he might figure out where to find them.

As he strolled along the road leading to his parents' house, John sensed the rightness of this moment. He was home. Lily was with him. That was how his life should be.

One of his mother's goats stood on the path in front of them and brayed a greeting.

"So cute," Lily said as she reached down to pat the short-haired brown-and-white spotted goat. "What's his name?"

"Her name. This is Honey. We've given up on trying to keep her penned. Honey thinks she owns the place."

"Haven't you told her that nobody owns the land?" Lily continued to scratch the Honey's forehead. "I've never actually seen a goat outside of a petting zoo."

"Don't make friends," he advised. "She'll follow you everywhere."

Lily stood up straighter and looked toward his parents' house. "Your sister lives here, too, right?"

"The baby of the family. She's in law school at the University of Denver."

"Do you have other brothers and sisters?"

"Two brothers who live in L.A. and one other sister who's married to a congressman from Wyoming."

"None of your family stayed on the reservation?"

"Some did, but most have moved away." He'd been among the first to go, joining the Marines so he'd have a chance for an education and training. The head injury and resulting temporary blindness were the price he'd had to pay, but he didn't regret the move. "I guess we were looking for a better life."

"Have you found it?"

"I like my job. My home." But he was missing an important piece that would make his life complete: a mate. He gazed into her upturned face. This little blond pixie was the woman he'd been waiting for.

Before they stepped onto the porch outside his parents' house, his mother was out the door, waving. She was a short, round woman who liked to dress in traditional clothing. Tonight, she wore a long, soft skirt and an orange blouse that made her resemble a pumpkin. She threw her arms around his neck and told him that she loved him.

When he introduced Lily, she got the same warm hug.

"Come inside." Yvonne Pinto held open the door. "I'm baking a pie."

"Pumpkin?" John asked.

"Apple. What made you think of pumpkins?"

"No reason."

Taking Lily's arm, he followed his mother into the house. His father stood in the door leading to the kitchen. "Come here, John. I want to show you something."

Beyond the living room was a huge kitchen. The large round table was covered with library books. His father pointed to a photograph of a giant sea turtle. "Did you see one of these on your trip?"

"Didn't have time. But we did see an iguana."

A frown creased his lined face. "The rock iguana or the blue?"

"I'm not one hundred percent sure." He pulled Lily forward. "Lily Clark, this is my father, Daniel."

She shook his hand. "I can see where John gets his love of research."

"On his travels, he should know where he's going and what he can learn." He cocked his head to one side and studied her. "You work with John. Are you a bodyguard?"

"I am," she said. "And I used to be a police officer."

He laughed. "Such a little thing. I bet you know kung fu."

"I could give you a demonstration," she offered. "Should I flip John onto his back?"

Yvonne bustled toward them. "No roughhousing in the kitchen. Sit at the table and push Daniel's books aside. We'll have pie with ice cream."

As she took a seat at the table, Lily couldn't help comparing this cluttered, cheerful household with her orderly childhood home where a twice-a-week cleaning person kept everything tidy and her mother posted a typed schedule of activities on a corkboard in the family room. Never had they eaten pie and ice cream before bedtime.

How ironic! Despite her careful upbringing, Lily was impulsive and rebellious. And John had emerged from this happy chaos to be a methodical planner.

She smiled at Yvonne. "I saw a loom in the living room. Do you weave rugs?"

"I learned from my mother, who learned from her mother and so on. I make some money with my rugs. Come. I'll show you."

Lily followed her into the living room while John and his father poured over the library books, trying to decide which type of iguana they'd sighted on Cuerva.

The living room showed a wide variety of interests. Books, magazines, an aquarium, a guitar and several herbs in painted clay pots. Yvonne's loom took up a lot of space. The half-finished wool rug was patterned in black, red and brown.

Deftly, she whipped a treadle through the vertical

strands. "I used to be more disciplined, but now I only work on my loom in the afternoon when I'm watching *Oprah*."

Lily enjoyed the incongruous notion of a Navajo woman practicing her ancient craft in front of the television. "I like your home. It's so alive."

"Like you," she said. "You have a spark, Lily. A bright flame. John sees it, too. He likes you."

"How can you tell?"

"He can't take his eyes away from you." Yvonne wrapped her in a hug. "Welcome to our family."

Lily wasn't sure how to react. Had she just been named an honorary member of the Pinto clan? "Um. Thank you."

"John is a good man. Even when he was a boy, he worked hard to help support the family. Sometimes, he's too serious. You'll be good for him. You'll make him laugh."

Moving way too fast. Within minutes of saying hello, Yvonne seemed to have them married off. She'd probably already picked out names for their children.

Still, Lily didn't want to disappoint this good-hearted lady. "Please don't get the wrong idea, Yvonne. John and I are only coworkers."

"But you went to the island together."

"We were on assignment." How could she explain without being crude? "We're not…dating."

"We'll see about that." Yvonne pursed her lips, then repeated, "We'll see."

After devouring a wedge of sugary, delicious apple pie and ice cream, Lily allowed John to drag her away. Walking away from his parents' house, she glanced back and saw Yvonne and Daniel standing on the porch, waving.

"They're terrific," she said.

"Never a dull moment."

Honey the goat fell into step behind them, and Lily encouraged her with another pat on the head. She liked having a pet goat. "For some reason, your mom seems to think we're having a relationship."

"She wants me to settle down."

As he walked, he hooked his thumbs in his belt loops and gazed up at the waning moon. His shining black hair fell loosely across his forehead. He looked young, almost boyish. But she knew John was in his late thirties. Experienced. Solid. Productive. "But you seem like you're very much settled down."

"Mom wants to see me married with half a dozen children. It's all about the grandbabies. I'm sure your mother is the same way."

"Hah!" She matched her pace to his easygoing gait. "My mother is a doctor. She wants me to have a meaningful career. Her message to me is that I'm too smart to settle for being a breeder."

"A breeder?"

"A woman who stays home, barefoot and pregnant." She glanced over her shoulder at Honey. "Raising goats."

"And what do you want, Lily?"

"I'm only twenty-six." She hadn't really thought about the long-term prospects. At the moment, her focus was on doing a good job at PPS. "I guess I want both. To be a kick-ass agent and to have babies."

"Yeah." John grinned. "Me, too."

A twig snapped. Immediately, John reacted. He turned toward the surrounding pine trees and placed himself in front of her, protecting her, reminding her that they weren't having a real relationship. They were together because of shared danger.

Quickly, he identified their intruder. "Deer."

Not as exotic as tripping over an iguana. "I didn't know they came this far down into the foothills."

"It's been a dry summer. They have to come to lower elevation looking for food."

They walked in silence. The closer they got to his house, the more she was thinking about what might happen tonight. Did he still want to make love to her?

It was a question she wanted to ask but didn't dare to speak aloud. She knew he liked her. When she thought of the kisses they'd shared, she knew they had chemistry. But he'd managed to go all these years without making a commitment. "Why haven't you gotten married?"

"Never found the right woman."

Lily frowned. She was making too much of this. Making love didn't mean a lifetime commitment. It was just sex. A biological function.

But not to me. She'd stayed a virgin all these years for a reason. Making love had to mean…something.

Chapter Fifteen

At John's house, Lily put off the decision about sleeping arrangements by retreating into the upstairs bathroom. She stood under the pulsating, detachable showerhead and allowed the steaming water to pelt her back and shoulders. If she could prolong this shower forever, she could avoid the inevitable moment when she stood face-to-face with John and told him that she preferred to sleep alone. But did she? Should she throw open her arms and say, "Take me, big boy?"

Remembering their fake lovemaking at the governor's mansion in Cuerva lightened her mood. Sex didn't have to be filled with angst and commitment. It could just be fun. *No big deal.* Why not make love with John?

Turning, she detached the showerhead and aimed the spray to hit on her collarbone. Rivulets of water coursed between her breasts. Her body was definitely ready for sex, tingling all over.

She heard a tap on the door. "Lily? Can I come in?"

"Sure." She was safely hidden behind a dark blue shower curtain.

She heard the door open and close. John said, "I have Evangeline on the phone. She needs more information on Ted Hawley. Do you remember what precinct he worked at?"

"I'm not sure. I think it was the west side of Denver. Near Invesco Field. He always got freebie tickets to the Bronco games."

John relayed the information into the phone. Inside the bathroom his voice echoed, and she liked the deep, masculine sound. Standing there, naked, she realized that she could get this party started by reaching through the shower curtain, grabbing his arm and pulling him under the water with her.

"Lily, can you think of any friends or associates of Ted Hawley? People he might be staying with?"

Needing to concentrate, she replaced the shower-head on the holder. Then she rattled off a few names. Former cop acquaintances. Guys she'd played basketball with. Being part of the Denver PD seemed like a lifetime ago.

She heard him say good-bye to Evangeline, heard the bathroom door open.

"Wait!" Impulsively, she peeked around the edge of the shower curtain. "Don't leave."

"Okay." He closed the door and replaced the receiver on the body of the telephone, disconnecting the call.

"What's with the old-fashioned phone?" she asked.

"A secure land line. Can't be traced." He waved through the steam. "Did you want something?"

Now or never. She grinned. "Care to join me?"

Without hesitation he kicked off his shoes and peeled off his socks. "Are you sure about this?"

"Maybe." She squashed the doubts that were swirling in her head. *No big deal.* This was going to be fun.

He unbuttoned his shirt and tossed it in a puddle on the floor. His bronzed chest beckoned to be touched. She thrust one hand out of the shower and crooked her finger. "Come here."

Steam from the shower gushed around them, but his flesh was cool and dry. He slid his arm around her, pulled her against him. With the shower curtain still between them, he tasted her lips. A delicious shiver went through her. Oh yes, she was sure that she wanted this. Wanted him. Wanted him naked.

Fighting the shower curtain, she groped for his belt. Her elbow hit the detachable showerhead, and it fell from its perch. Water sprayed wildly. She ought to grab it, but she was single-mindedly struggling with his belt buckle. Oh, hell. This was a mess. Her worst fear realized. Not only was she an inexperienced lover but also a klutz. So clumsy. She'd turned what should have been a beautiful moment of lovemaking into a joke.

But John wasn't laughing. He stepped into the tub, still wearing his now-drenched khaki trousers, picked up the showerhead and held her. Her breasts flattened against his chest. Her naked body molded against him. "You're all wet," she gasped.

"So are you."

He directed the spray against her spine. The heat from the water spiraled through her. Her front side pressed hard against him. "John?"

"Yes, Lily?"

"Is that a wallet in your pocket or are you happy to see me?"

"You know what it is," he said. "I'm very happy."

He separated from her. His gaze slid over her like warm honey—slow and sweet. He cupped her breasts and dipped his head to taste her hard nipples. Electricity jolted through her.

Then he turned her around, facing the wall with the shower faucets. She braced herself with her hands on the white tiles. His hand glided down her torso and the flare of her hips. With one arm around her waist, he held her. She couldn't move. Didn't want to.

With the other hand, he reached around her with the showerhead, focused the spray on her breasts. The sharp water darts pricked against her. Then he directed the spray down her stomach and lower.

Her breath caught. Powerful sensations were building inside her. She parted her legs, welcoming the pulsating spray.

The tingling became a spasm that rocked her body. Her eyelids squeezed shut. She heard herself moaning, gasping. Every muscle in her body tensed. Goose bumps quivered on skin. Sensation exploded in sweet release.

This was it—the thing her girlfriends had told her

about but couldn't explain. An orgasm. But she was still, technically, a virgin.

With her eyes still closed, she wrenched free from his restraint and flung her arms around his neck. Vaguely, she was aware of the shower being turned off.

John helped her out of the tub, wrapped her in a fluffy towel.

Her knees felt weak, but he wouldn't let her fall. She trusted him implicitly. When she opened her eyes, he was naked. His body was magnificent.

She should have been embarrassed, but that was the furthest thing from her mind as he opened the bathroom door, lifted her into his arms and carried her down the hall to his bedroom.

They were between the sheets. Under a forest-green down comforter. This time, their lovemaking would be for real.

She snuggled up to him, enjoying the feel of his hard, hot erection pressing against her belly. In his dark eyes, she saw strength, masculine confidence. The man knew what he was doing. "You're good at this."

"So are you."

"Me? I was just standing there."

"Not true. Your body is sensitive. Beautiful. Hot." He cupped her butt, fitting her more tightly against him. "There's nothing more arousing to a man than a woman who enjoys sex."

"But I'm a virgin."

"Not for long."

"I'm so ready." She glided her hand down his

body to touch his hard shaft. "When you talked about making love, you made a lot of promises."

"Trust me, Lily. You won't be disappointed."

She believed him. One hundred percent. And she gave herself over to him, learning the sensitive secrets that had been locked inside her, reveling in each trembling pleasure. When he finally sheathed himself in a condom and penetrated her, she felt fulfillment. An amazing sense of rightness. Almost like destiny. This was meant to happen in this time, in this place, with this man. This incredible, fantastic man.

AT THREE O'CLOCK IN THE morning, John was wakened by the buzz of the secure phone at his bedside. He flung out an arm and grabbed the receiver on his secure land line. "What?"

"It's Robert."

In an instant, John was completely awake. He yanked his arm out from under Lily and sat up on the bed. If Robert was calling in the middle of the night, it meant trouble. "What's up?"

"I have deciphered part of this information we downloaded from the computer at Bank St. George. It seems that Clive Fuentes is in Spain. At least, I've narrowed the search to one country. And I have the list of investors translated into a string of numbers and letters. Unfortunately, I can't figure out how they break into names."

"Are you in danger?" John asked.

"Certainly not. I'm at the safe house. Everything is fine."

Then why the hell was he calling? John appreciated the update, but it could have waited until morning. He rubbed a hand across his forehead and glanced over at Lily, who had, once again taken all the covers and bunched them around her side of the bed. Still asleep, she was smiling. Satisfied. And so was he.

He spoke quietly into the phone. "Robert, I'm not a decryption expert. Contact Cassie. She figured out that list of land coordinates you sent. She's damn good. And she knows computers."

"As did Lenny."

They shared a moment of silence in Lenny's memory. John sensed that Robert hadn't really called to talk about decryption. These lonely hours between midnight and dawn were the time when anxieties appeared. "Have you been thinking about Lenny?"

"I deeply regret his murder." Robert's usually crisp British accent sounded blurred. "Can't help feeling that it was my fault."

Not wanting to awaken Lily, John picked up the phone. The extra-long cord stretched across the bedroom to the sliding glass door that opened onto the long balcony above the front porch.

Outside, he shivered in the cool night air. Probably should have grabbed a robe. "You can't blame yourself, Robert."

"It all ties back to Clive Fuentes. My nemesis."

"And you're a victim, too. He sabotaged your airplane, drove you undercover for two years."

"I keep imagining Lenny's death. Being blown to bits by a Molotov cocktail at a gas station. Horrible."

Everyone at PPS mourned Lenny. He was a sweet guy, an innocent. "I'm pretty sure that Ted Hawley is responsible for Lenny's murder. Hawley likes to use bombs. He kept trying to qualify for a SWAT team but didn't have the smarts."

"Is Hawley back in Denver?"

"Don't know. Evangeline has people working on locating him."

John looked down from his balcony to the peaceful mountain valley. All the lights were out in his parents' house. And at the Iron Deer residence. He straightened his shoulders and embraced the starry night. The chill reminded him that he was still alive. It felt good to be home again. With Lily in his bed.

Robert croaked, "How is she? Evangeline?"

"Haven't you spoken to her? The phones in the safe house are totally secure."

"I won't take that risk. If there's the slightest hint that I'm back in Denver, everyone will be in danger."

"You covered that base," John reminded him. Robert was being entirely irrational. "You made that call to the governor and told him that if anyone else was hurt, the money would be gone forever."

"When you talked to Evangeline, what did she say?"

"She wanted to know how you were, and I told her."

"Yes? What did you say?"

Annoyed by how these two adults were tiptoeing around each other like a couple of teenagers, John shook his head. "I told her that you were the same cranky old dodger that you always were. Maybe with a few more gray hairs and a few more ribs sticking out on your scrawny body. You have to face her, Robert. Tomorrow. Do you want me to arrange it?"

"Yes," he said. "And there's one more thing. It occurred to me that Peter Turner might have the key to unlocking this encryption."

John remembered how the single word Peter had communicated was responsible for getting final access to the computer files. "I'll go to the hospital tomorrow and pay him a visit."

"Thank you, John."

"Get some sleep."

When he returned to the bedroom, Lily was sitting up on the bed, waiting for him with the bedside lamp turned on. "Is something wrong?"

He set down the phone and dove under the comforter. He wrapped an arm around her and rested his cold cheek on her warm, pliant breast.

She let out a shriek and shoved him away. "You're an ice cube."

"It's your job to warm me up." He flopped his arm across her again.

"My job?"

With an amazing and determined burst of energy, she dodged out from under his arm, flipped him onto his back, straddled his torso and threw a hold on his throat. "Remember the Vulcan Death Grip? I can have you unconscious in twelve seconds."

"Well, now," he drawled. "I'm really scared."

"You better be."

He looked up at her lovely, vivacious face. The

angle of her chin. Her slender throat. His gaze slid happily down to her breasts and lower to her spread thighs. "Have you got me where you want me?"

As she settled on top of him, he heard a rumble in her throat. Almost like purring. "I do want you. Again."

"Good." Because he was already hard.

"But first, I want you to tell me what that phone call was about."

"Robert. Trying to figure out the downloaded information." He glided his hand along the smooth contours of her back. "But that's not really why he called. He's nervous about seeing Evangeline again."

"I can understand that."

"Yeah? Explain it to me."

"If I were Evangeline," Lily said, "I'd be angry. Of course, Robert felt like he was doing the right thing by staying away and keeping everything top secret. But she has to be thinking that he could have figured something out. He could have found his way back to her."

"But now they'll be together," John said. "Happy ending. Right?"

"I hope so. But people can change in two years."

"Not Robert and Evangeline." He'd seen them together. A couple who were perfectly suited, completely in love. "They're meant to be together."

Like us. He was meant to be with Lily. They shared the same interests, wanted the same things. Making love to her convinced him. She was the woman for him. His woman. His destiny.

He rolled her onto her back and kissed her, long

and hard. Her soft moan aroused him. When he looked down at her, he saw perfection.

Tomorrow, he would tell her. And they would make plans for their future together.

Chapter Sixteen

In the morning, Lily leaned against the porch railing at John's house, smiling for no particular reason and watching the antics of Honey, who marched back and forth in front of the house with a deflated football in her mouth. *So cute.* Lily's smile spread through her whole body. Though the weather was ordinary, it felt like she was floating on pink fluffy clouds. If she'd known sex could be this fantastic, she wouldn't have waited so long.

As far as she could tell, there was no down side. She'd been prepared for soreness; other women had told her she'd be sore. Hah! This tiny ache was nothing compared to the bruises from surviving their plane crash into the Caribbean.

Her lips were a little swollen from the ten million kisses they'd shared last night, but she didn't think she really looked any different. Same face. Same nose. Same hair.

When John stepped outside and joined her, she asked, "Do you think anyone will notice?"

"Notice what?"

"That I'm not a virgin anymore."

He snuggled an arm around her waist. "If you want, we could get you a tattoo. The letter *V* with a line through it."

"And where would I put this tattoo?"

He slipped his hand down the front of her T-shirt and tweaked the edge of her bra. "Right here. This is a nice, soft, creamy spot."

She loved the way she felt when he touched her. "Okay."

"You know, Lily, you really shouldn't be standing out here alone."

"I'm not alone." She pointed to the goat who dropped the smashed football and brayed.

"Seriously," he said. "We need to be careful until we're sure there isn't a threat."

"Did I mention that last night was amazing?" She sighed. "I guess I did mention it. About a hundred times. I think we should do it again tonight."

"Tonight and tomorrow night." He tightened his grasp around her midsection and squeezed. "And many tomorrows to come."

"That sounds like a long time."

"Forever," he said simply.

Forever? An alarm bell went off in the back of her mind. John wasn't the type of guy who threw words around lightly. Some of his language was profound, like when he said that no one could own the earth. But he wasn't a poet who dropped colorful phrases that rang like ballad lyrics. When he said "forever," he probably meant it literally. A dictionary definition. Forever, as in extending into the foreseeable future.

Surely, he didn't mean it. But what if he did? What if he had decided it was time to take his mother's advice to settle down and produce grand-babies. With her?

Forever? She saw herself in the kitchen, hugely pregnant. Another child tugged at her skirt. She was baking a pie. Watching the soaps on television. She'd become a breeder.

"Forever, huh?" She cleared her throat, which had suddenly become tight. "Coming from a confirmed bachelor like you, that sounds awfully close to a commitment."

"People change."

She eyed him curiously. Some people changed. But not him. John was methodical, steady and stable. He didn't make spontaneous leaps into the unknown. What was he planning?

He checked his wristwatch. "We should leave now. Ready?"

"Right." Time to set aside her personal concerns and to mentally change gears. Floating around inside her head didn't encourage the sharp, alert manner necessary for a PPS agent. She was already wearing her ankle holster. Her wallet was in her pocket. She slipped on her sunglasses. "What's our agenda for today?"

"First, the hospital where we'll visit Peter Turner. He's out of the coma and on his way to complete recovery."

"And what are we looking for?"

"Robert wants us to find out if Peter knows anything that might help decipher the code. But we need to be careful talking to him so we don't put him in danger."

"How careful?"

"Assume that his hospital room is bugged. Or that one of his nurses is on Kirshner's payroll. Anybody could be listening."

"Like in Cuerva."

"Speaking of Cuerva," he said. "If anybody asks, we had a great little vacation. No details."

"Got it." They should operate under the assumption that they were under surveillance at all times. "Where do we go after the hospital?"

"Check in at the PPS office, debrief our real experiences at Cuerva."

"Then Evangeline wants us to take a week off, right?"

"Not quite," he said. "We still have to arrange the logistics for a time and place when Mr. and Mrs. Prescott can finally get together."

Robert and Evangeline were making this meeting too complicated. With the resources of PPS at their disposal, they could be well protected anywhere.

But Lily was willing to cut them some slack. Evangeline probably wouldn't want to see her husband for the first time in two years with a phalanx of bodyguards surrounding them. And Robert had been hiding out for two years, which was enough to make anyone paranoid.

"After the office, can we swing by my apartment?" She looked down at the plain black T-shirt she'd been wearing for two days. "I need to pick up some fresh clothes. I've been wearing these jeans so long that they can probably walk to the closet by themselves."

"Let's get an update on Hawley first."

Though she'd brushed off his earlier comment about the threat, she hadn't forgotten. Hawley could be anywhere. Watching and waiting for the time when he would strike out at her. Not a pleasant thought.

She felt the smile fading from her lips. Her fluffy pink clouds were being chased away by impending thunderheads.

ON A HILL ACROSS THE STREET from the hospital parking lot, Ted Hawley adjusted his binoculars. He wished he could get closer, but the lot and hospital had video surveillance. And PPS knew his identity. He couldn't take a chance on being spotted.

How the hell would he ever go back to being a cop? As soon as he returned to the station, Lily would finger him. There was nothing she could prove. Even that final shootout on Cuerva was her word against his. But there would be an Internal Affairs investigation, and that might be enough to get him discharged.

What did he care? He was making three times as much with this undercover stuff than he ever made walking a beat. But he liked being a cop, having the respect that came with wearing a badge.

He focused on a silver mid-sized sedan that pulled into a space in the third row. He'd planned this stakeout for visiting hours when PPS agents were likely to stop by and spend some time with Peter Turner—the half brother of Kyle Prescott, Robert Prescott's son. A couple of spoiled rich kids, they were next in line to inherit the TCM empire.

The car doors opened on the silver sedan. He saw the sunlight reflecting off Lily's short blond hair. The bitch was back in town.

She hadn't gone to her apartment last night. He knew because he'd been watching. She must be staying with the boyfriend. They were holding hands as they walked into the hospital.

On the car seat beside him was a semiautomatic pistol. He wanted to open fire right now, to charge down this hill like vengeance unleashed and put a hole in her forehead. The woman was a burr on his ass. Always in the way. She was going to cost him his job. She needed to be taken out of the way.

She wasn't his primary target, but Lily would be useful to him in locating Robert Prescott. She could be his hostage. He'd squeeze her until she broke, giving him the information he needed.

He could pull this off. He had the SWAT team training and the equipment he needed for a full assault. Nobody could stop him.

JOHN AND LILY FOUND OTHER visitors in Peter Turner's private hospital room on the third floor. Though the room was fairly large, with two beds and a long window looking out at the foothills, the space seemed crowded. In a glance, John acknowledged Sara

Montgomery from PPS and Kyle Prescott. It was obvious that the two of them had become a couple. A handsome couple. Well matched and poised.

Propped against the pillows on his hospital bed, Peter looked exhausted. His wan complexion faded into his pale blond hair. Holding his hand was Angel, the gum-chewing Goth receptionist from PPS.

She bounced to her feet as soon as she spotted John and Lily. After quick hugs, she squinted at them and pursed her lips, which were outlined in black. "How come you don't have sunburns? How can anybody go to the Caribbean and not get out in the sun?"

Angel's white complexion, contrasted with black hair and eye makeup, made her comment particularly ironic.

"Do you ever tan?" John asked.

Her frown deepened. "Not my thing."

Lily said, "I didn't know you and Peter were acquainted."

"I'm helping him." She snapped her ever-present gum and returned to the bedside. "I brought this magical balm. It's made of St. John's wort, dill weed and some really fierce Chinese herbs."

She held up a brown vial. "Smell it."

Lily went first. "Lilacs?"

"Yeah!" Angel bobbed her head, sending her long silver earrings jangling. "I thought so, too. One of those Chinese names must mean lilac. I've been rubbing it into Peter's hand."

When John glanced at the patient, Peter mouthed the words, *Help me*.

Angel patted his shoulder. "Poor Peter has lost his memory, and this balm is going to help him remember."

Lily scooted up to the bedside. "You have amnesia, Peter?"

"The doctor said short-term memory loss is typical after a severe head trauma."

"It'll all come back," Angel assured him as she circled to the other side of the bed. "Don't you worry. I'll get started on this other hand."

A little nurse in patterned scrubs marched into the room and announced, "Too many visitors. You're quite a popular guy, Peter, but we can't be having parties in the room. Two of you have to leave."

Kyle Prescott stepped forward. "John and I will go. I'm sure Peter would rather be surrounded by beautiful women than be with us."

Before leaving the room, he met the gaze of his half brother. "You're going to be okay, Peter."

"Damn straight," Peter said.

Walking down the hospital corridor with Kyle, John noted how much this young man resembled his father. Like Robert, Kyle was tall and lean. His bright blue eyes reflected his father's sharp intelligence.

In the waiting area at the end of the corridor, they faced each other. John asked, "How is Peter really doing?"

"He's expected to make a full recovery." Kyle glanced down the corridor, then looked back at John. "My mother was supposed to be here a half hour ago to talk to the doctors."

John hoped he'd be gone before Olivia showed. "Tell me about Peter's amnesia."

"His memory is fuzzy. Head injuries are unpredictable."

As John well knew. "When Peter was coming in and out of his coma, he communicated one word. *Coyote.* Did he ever explain that word or say anything more about it?"

"Afraid not. If you're looking for useful information from my brother, you're out of luck." Kyle met his gaze, confronted him directly. "I know my father is alive."

There was no point in denying it. Even Robert's enemies knew he was alive. "Yes."

"Is he well?"

John nodded. "As well as can be expected."

"I want to see him."

He remembered Kyle's genuine grief at the memorial service for his father. Though the young man hadn't outright sobbed or made a public display, sorrow had weighed upon him, slumping his shoulders and dimming the light in his eyes. John knew from conversations with Robert that there were many regrets in this strained father-son relationship. Too many words not spoken. Too much pain unexpressed.

For one thing, Kyle had spent too many years with Robert's ex-wife, Olivia, and her husband, Stephen Turner, the CEO of Tri Corps. Media. Until the recent murders and the PPS investigations, Kyle was being groomed to take over the TCM businesses.

"John, is he here? Is my father in Denver?"

"Even if he were, I couldn't tell you."

"Because you don't trust me?"

"I know you'd never do anything to hurt your father." His gaze scanned the corridor, noting the presence of nurses in scrubs, patients and visitors. There were always too many people wandering around in a hospital. Too many ears to overhear. "This isn't a secure place to talk."

"When?"

"You'll have answers soon. Very soon."

The determined set of Kyle's jaw was exactly like his father. "I intend to find out where he is and to make things right between us."

It was a shame that it took losing his father for Kyle to acknowledge how much he cared. Robert would be deeply gratified to patch up the relationship. "When I saw your father, the first thing he asked about was you."

Kyle looked down at the tips of his shoes. "When he was here in town, we barely talked. Then, I thought he was dead. And I had so much I wanted to say. I've been a disappointment."

"Never think that," John said. "Your father blames himself more than you."

Frankly, John believed that the estrangement of father and son was caused by a force outside both of them: Olivia. She was a high-maintenance woman with the ethics of a garden slug. Olivia wouldn't hesitate to bad-mouth Robert to his son.

When he looked up and saw her stalking down the

corridor, he struggled to keep his expression neutral. Picking a fight with Olivia wouldn't help anything.

She came to a halt a few feet away from him and Kyle. Striking a model's pose, she rested one manicured hand on her thin hip. John didn't know much about women's fashion, but he could tell that her dress was high quality and her diamond bracelet was the real thing. Her curly dark hair framed an expressionless face. When she removed her sunglasses, her eyes flashed like emeralds and then went cold as stone.

Without a hint of a smile, she said, "How lovely to see you, John."

"Same here."

"I've heard some rather disturbing rumors," she said. "Rumors that Robert faked his own death. You wouldn't happen to know anything about that, would you?"

"It's better if I say nothing."

"Better for who? Evangeline?" She bared her teeth in an imitation of a smile. "This is so very typical. You all huddle around, protecting her. And nobody cares about me. My son is almost killed and nobody pays the least bit of attention."

"That's not true," Kyle said calmly. "People from PPS have stopped by almost every day to check on Peter."

"We're talking about me, dear." She placed her hand on her chest. "A mother's pain and suffering."

It was hard to believe this self-centered woman had actually given birth, but John was willing to give her some leeway. Peter had been in a coma and near death. No parent—not even Olivia—should have to face their child's mortality. "I'm sorry for what you went through, Olivia. And I'm very glad that Peter is getting better."

"Thank you, John."

When she turned on her heel and strode to Peter's room, John was tempted to run in the opposite direction, but he still had to get Lily. Reluctantly, he dragged himself down the hall in Olivia's wake, hoping that she'd finished with him.

No such luck. At the door to Peter's room, she whirled and glared at him. Her voice was a harsh whisper. "You can tell your precious friend Robert that he should have stayed dead. He played a cruel trick on us. I don't want to see him again. Neither does Kyle."

Kyle had overheard. "Stop it, Mother. You don't speak for me."

A strangled laugh tore through her lips. "Of course not. What was I thinking? Silly me."

She rushed into Peter's room, issuing orders with every step. Close the curtains. Straighten the sheets. Fluff the pillows.

The message was clear: Olivia was here, and she was in charge. She seated herself on the bed beside Peter in an artful pose and shot an angry, imperious gaze at all of them. "Leave us," she said.

The queen had spoken.

Even for Olivia, this was manic, crazy behavior. John took Lily's arm as he directed her from the room. He would never understand why Robert had married that woman.

Chapter Seventeen

In the rental car, John headed toward the downtown offices of PPS. Beside him in the passenger seat, Lily fidgeted, which he figured was a natural reaction to meeting Olivia for the first time.

Automatically, he checked his rearview mirror to make sure they weren't being followed. In the city, it was hard to tell. Too much traffic. Too many cars.

He wouldn't be surprised if they had picked up a tail at the hospital. Kirshner was looking for them, and half the staff at PPS seemed to regularly visit Peter. It was a logical assumption that John and Lily might turn up there.

"That was a waste of time," he said. "Peter doesn't have a clue about the list of investors."

"If he really has amnesia," she said. "His memory loss seems much too convenient."

He glanced over at her. Like a well-trained agent, her gaze was constantly in motion, checking out the side-view mirror and the cars around them. "You think Peter is hiding something."

"He knows more than he's telling," she said. "He had the secret password to get inside the computer system at Bank St. George."

At one time, Peter Turner had been under suspicion. Through his connections and his work at TCM, he was linked to Kingston Investment and Trust. "If he was against Robert, why would he pass along that important bit of information?"

"He wasn't fully out of his coma. I think he wants to cooperate. His heart is in the right place and his instincts are telling him that he wants to be on our side. But he's aware of the danger."

"Now that he's more alert," John concluded, "he's hiding behind memory loss to protect himself. Or someone else."

"Like his father?"

Stephen Turner—another relatively sane-appearing man who had married Olivia and had had a son with her—had been cooperating with the PPS investigation. "We won't know until Robert gets that list decrypted."

Lily huffed out a little sigh. Her hand slid down her leg to adjust her ankle holster. Fidgeting.

"Something bothering you?" he asked.

"Earlier, you said something about forever."

"That's right." He remembered the moment with pleasure. "You and me. Making love forever."

"What did you mean by that? Exactly."

When he pulled up at a stoplight and looked over at her, her fidgets had increased to outright nervousness. She tapped her fingers on her thigh as if she were playing "The Minute Waltz" on a keyboard. "*Forever* means that I want to spend time with you. A lot of time."

"But you weren't talking about, you know, a commitment. Or a relationship. Or even—I know this is ridiculous—something like marriage."

If she'd actually been playing a piano, he would have heard a dark, minor chord. "Why is the idea of marriage ridiculous?"

"Well, it just is." Her shoulders twitched. "I'm only twenty-six, and I love working at PPS. You wouldn't want to be married to somebody who carries a gun. You're looking for a woman who's ready to settle down and have babies."

Where the hell had she gotten that idea? "Having babies is what my mother wants. Not my number one priority."

"Good," she said. "I want to make it clear that you aren't thinking about anything permanent. Like marriage."

Getting married wasn't out of the question. He'd considered the idea. After last night, John was fairly sure that Lily was the woman he'd been waiting for, the woman he wanted to spend the rest of his life with. Clearly, that meant commitment. And, very likely, marriage.

This wasn't the way he intended to mention that topic. He wasn't about to propose between stoplights on Santa Fe Drive.

His cell phone rang. *Saved by the bell.* He pulled it out of his pocket and answered.

"I need to see Evangeline now."

"Robert?" John was shocked by the sound of his voice. Why the hell was he calling on an unsecured line? They'd gone to a lot of trouble to make sure nobody could track his location. "Where are you?"

"On my way into town."

"That's suicide."

"I decrypted the list," he said. "I have the names and I need to—"

"Stop!" John interrupted. "Don't say one more goddamned word over this phone. We could be monitored."

The chances of picking up his cell phone transmission in the middle of Denver were slim, but he didn't want to risk it. Robert had spent two years undercover, carefully tracking this thread of investors that led back to Clive Fuentes. They'd broken into a bank to get the list. Why was he throwing away two years of intense investigation?

Firmly, John said, "You can't come into town."

"The last time I checked, my name was on the letterhead at Prescott Personal Securities."

John couldn't believe he was playing the boss card. They worked together as a team. "And that's what you told the agents who were watching you at the safe house. You're the boss."

"Correct."

"That doesn't fly with me. I've known you too long." Every minute they were on the phone increased the chances of someone getting a signal to locate Robert's position. "I'm not afraid to tell you that you're doing something stupid. Taking a risk that could put other people in danger. You haven't come this far to blow it."

"Perhaps I'm not being rational."

"I am," John said. "Trust me, Robert. I'm always rational."

"Yes, you are."

"Go to the tribe," John said, referring to his mountain home. Robert had been there several times and commented on how John had established his own tribe in Colorado. "Do you understand?"

"Yes."

"Turn off your cell phone. Better yet, throw the damn thing out the window. The signal could be traced."

"As usual, John, you're making sense. But there's one thing I must say before I disconnect. The list of investors included the name of every murder victim. Clive must be systematically killing them off to get complete control of the money."

It was a hit list. By eliminating investors in the blind trust—names that couldn't be traced until they broke into the bank and got the list—Clive was making himself richer. There might even be some sort of insurance scam involved with each death. "Is Drew Kirshner on that list?"

"He is. But the very next name," Robert said, "is Evangeline."

No wonder he'd been frantic. "I'll warn her."

"And I will join the tribe."

The phone went dead in his hand.

Crossing two lanes of traffic, John turned west toward his home.

"What's going on?" Lily asked.

"Robert has the list of names figured out. The murder victims are on it. And so is Evangeline."

"How could that be? Wouldn't she know if she was part of Kingston Trust and Investment?"

"High finance." Definitely not John's area of expertise. "Robert is a wealthy man with investments all around the globe. And Clive used to be his friend. His mentor. I'm guessing that Robert trusted Clive to make some investments for him, and Clive funneled Robert's money through channels until he ended up in this blind trust."

"But how does that affect Evangeline?"

"When Robert was declared dead, his assets passed to her."

He gripped the steering wheel, frustrated by a slowdown in traffic. He needed speed. Needed to reach Robert in time, get him to somewhere safe. And Evangeline, too.

"We need to warn her," Lily said. "If she's in the PPS offices, she's safe. Our security is top-notch. But we need to make sure she stays there."

"Call her on my cell phone, then turn it off."

He had kept his older-model cell phone specifically because it lacked the GPS tracer that had become standard in some of the newer models. When turned off, no signal was emitted.

"What should I tell her?"

"We're picking up Robert at my house. Once

we've got him, we'll call her again. We need a safe destination."

The traffic jam cleared, and he sped west. The location of his house was a rural route—obscure enough that delivery men regularly got lost trying to find him. But it wasn't a safe house. There were maps. It could be found.

Lily ended her conversation and turned off his phone. "I've never heard Evangeline sound like that. She's really upset. Why would Robert go crazy like that?"

"He's not thinking," John said. "He's listening only to his heart. Evangeline is under mortal threat, and her safety is more important to him than his own life. His love is a powerful force that can't be explained or measured."

"But he held himself back, stayed away from her for two whole years."

"He's at the end of his restraint." John knew what it meant to hold back and be cautious, to keep his emotions tightly wrapped. "Evangeline is everything to him. That's how I feel about you, Lily."

"You do?"

From the first time he kissed her at the airport in Jamaica, he had sensed a bond. Last night, their lovemaking forged their connection.

He whipped the rental car into the fast lane. The highway was a straight line leading into the mountains. If anyone was following them on the highway, John had only one evasive tactic. "You're the woman I want to spend my life with."

"Now isn't the time to talk about this."

It was the only time. "I didn't plan to say this now. But I want to marry you, Lily. I want your life to be one with mine. Say you'll be my wife."

"I can't answer that. You're being unreasonable."

She was right. And he didn't care. For once in his well-organized life, he had no backup plan. She was all that mattered to him, and he needed to seal that bond. "If you can't marry me, it's best that we end this now."

He couldn't take his eyes off the road to see her reaction. It was time to make the move that would throw off anyone pursuing them. "Hang on, Lily."

He floored the accelerator. Raced past a semi-truck. Cranked the steering wheel hard right and made the exit with only inches to spare. Anyone following them would have to go all the way up to the next exit and double back.

Unless there was a second car. Unless someone was already at the exit waiting. Or waiting at the house. Second thoughts clicked through his mind. Had he misread the situation?

He glanced over at Lily. He might have made the worst mistake of his life.

IN SPITE OF HER SEAT BELT, Lily was thrown against the passenger door as their rental car raced up the exit and turned south. They were flying, moving fast, darting around slower vehicles in classic evasive maneuvers. "Are we being tailed?"

"I'm assuming that we are."

"Why?"

"Revenge," he said. "We were with Robert when he robbed Bank St. George."

"Good reason."

"Also, anybody looking for Robert would figure that we'd know where he is. We're the link."

She unholstered her gun and turned in her seat to watch the road behind them. John swerved off the two-lane road into a stand of pine and cottonwood. He cut the engine and waited, watching as several vehicles passed at regular speed.

In spite of the sunlit July day, the silence looming between them felt as cold as the belly of a glacier. She should have been concentrating on spotting a tail. Instead, it took all her willpower to control the frustration and anger surging inside her. She wanted to scream.

How could he toss out that ultimatum? Marry me or else. Damn it, that wasn't fair. Why? Why couldn't they be like a normal couple?

They should have built their relationship during a couple months of dating. Gone to movies. Exchanged Valentine's Day presents.

They hadn't even spoken the "L" word. And he expected her to respond to a marriage proposal?

She peered through the windshield as other traffic drove lazily past. She didn't have to look at John to feel his intensity. He was so much a part of her that she imagined she could hear the strong, steady beat of his heart.

Nothing about this relationship was normal.

They'd survived a plane crash and robbed a bank. And they'd made love. For the first time in her life, she'd given herself to a man, and it had been more than she'd ever expected.

But did she love John? Was she experienced enough to know? She cared for him. That was for damn sure. When she looked at him, she felt a thrill of unexplainable joy. The thought of losing him caused a physical ache in her stomach.

But she wouldn't be forced into marriage.

If he pressed for her answer, it had to be no. She had to say goodbye.

Chapter Eighteen

On the last miles to his house, neither of them spoke. Lily trained her focus on her job. Watching for danger. When they pulled up in front of John's house, she didn't see another car parked outside. "Did we get here before Robert?"

"He probably parked around back. He's been here before." John opened his car door quickly. "We need to move fast. There are too many places in the forest for a sniper to hide."

Gun in hand, she hit the porch at a dead run. Robert came around the side of the house and joined them. John hustled them both inside and punched the deactivate code into the security alarm.

They stood inside the doorway, breathing hard. Apprehension surrounded them. Though she was furious at Robert for putting them all in danger, she couldn't help feeling sorry for him. His face was even more gaunt than before. Dark circles underlined his bright blue eyes. The man looked like he hadn't slept all night.

"Evangeline," he said. "Is she safe?"

"I spoke to her," Lily said. "She's at PPS. As you know, the security in the office is tight as a fist."

John stepped away from their threesome, distancing himself. His jaw was set. His eye was steady. Damn, he was handsome.

"Here's an idea," he said coldly. "I have a secure phone line here, Robert. Why don't you go upstairs to my bedroom and call Evangeline yourself?"

"I should."

"Good. Because I'm done with being your go-between."

Stiffly, he strode toward the kitchen, not bothering to look back over his shoulder. She had the feeling that if she or Robert said anything, John would literally explode.

Robert turned toward her. "Please excuse me. I need to telephone my wife."

As he ascended the staircase to the second floor, Lily went into the kitchen where John was making a pot of coffee. Without facing her, he said, "Standard lookout procedure. I'll keep an eye on the front of the house. You watch the back."

They needed to talk. She couldn't stand this pressure.

"The best vantage point," he said, "is the kitchen window by the door. But move around. Go from window to window. Don't follow a predictable pattern."

When he turned toward her, their gazes locked. She saw turmoil in his eyes—a dark confusion that was completely unlike him. His unanswered question hung in the air between them. Would she marry him?

"John, I can't—"

He silenced her with a kiss, yanked her into his arms with such force that her feet left the floor. His mouth was hot, demanding, persuasive. He took her breath away. She couldn't resist. He was too strong, too fierce.

She wanted his kisses to go on…forever.

They weren't a normal couple. They were better.

She pressed hard against him, wrapped her legs around his thighs, climbed him like a tree. He leaned her against the countertop. There was nothing sweet and gentle about this embrace. She wanted him desperately.

She heard Robert enter the kitchen. "Evangeline's gone," he said.

She and John broke apart. "What?"

"Gone," Robert repeated. "She doesn't answer her phone. Angel said she left the office."

Still reeling from their kiss, Lily untangled herself from John's grasp. She didn't completely comprehend what Robert was saying.

"Calm down," John said. "She must have gone underground to a safe place."

None of them believed his words. Evangeline was a sensible woman, trained by the FBI at Quantico, smart enough to know that the PPS offices offered total protection. But Angel said she'd left. On her own. Where would she go? It was out of character for her to take an unnecessary risk.

Lily mentally replayed her conversation with Evangeline, trying to remember if she'd said anything that would indicate her whereabouts. All Lily could remember was Evangeline's concern about Robert. Was he well? How did he look?

"We have to find her." Robert's exhaustion had caught up with him. His hands trembled at his sides. "If anything happens to her, my life is over."

John straightened his shoulders. "We need a plan."

If the situation hadn't been so dire, she would have laughed out loud. In any given disaster, John would turn to logic. Even though this situation made no rational sense. "Have you got any ideas?"

"Not yet."

"Well, let's just look at the facts," she said. "All the people affected when we robbed the bank want us dead. Hawley and Kirshner are coming after us. Evangeline is on the run. And somewhere in Spain…" She turned to Robert. "That's right, isn't it? Clive Fuentes is in Spain?"

He nodded.

She continued, "…somewhere in Spain, Clive Fuentes is laughing his butt off."

"That's fairly accurate," John said.

"We're swirling at the edge of the toilet bowl," she said. "All we can do is tread water."

John shrugged. "At least, things can't get worse."

He was wrong.

There was a blast of gunfire. The front door crashed open. A piercing alarm sounded.

John reacted quickly. At the back door, he punched in a code to shut off the alarm.

She grabbed Robert's arm and pulled him to the floor.

He wrenched away from her. "I can handle this. I'm armed."

"They're after you, Robert. You're the prize. Stay out of sight."

"The hell I will."

He rose unsteadily to his feet. Though she had to admire his determination, he'd get them all killed if he showed himself. He straightened his shoulders. "I'll take care of this."

John came up beside him. With one quick jab, he knocked his boss unconscious and hauled his slumping body into the pantry.

Gun in hand, she peeked around the door jamb.

Standing in the center of the living room was Drew Kirshner. His sports jacket was torn, and he looked like he'd been beaten. His shirt was bloody. His eyes, terrified.

Behind him was a man holding a repeating rifle. He was dressed head-to-toe in a helmet and body armor. She couldn't see his face, but this had to be Ted Hawley. He'd always wanted to be on a SWAT team.

"Throw down your weapons," he said. "Or I kill this son of a bitch. You've got three seconds."

"I don't have my gun," Lily shouted back. "I was in the kitchen getting a cup of coffee. Can't you smell it?"

Hawley probably couldn't smell anything behind the bullet-proof Plexiglas face mask attached to his helmet. The body armor presented a problem. Even if hit in the arm or leg, he could still squeeze off several fatal rounds.

Lily knew she had to keep him talking, keep him distracted. "Can I bring you a cup of coffee? It's fresh."

"I didn't come here for a damn beverage."

She heard a spray of bullets, the sound of shattering pottery, Kirshner's whimpering pleas.

John crept up behind Lily. "The alarm is still ringing through to the police station. They'll be here."

"How long?"

"I'll stall him," John said. "You go out the kitchen door and circle around front. You can surprise him from behind. Aim for his legs."

"Show yourself," Hawley yelled. "Come out with both hands up."

John tucked his gun into the back waistband of his jeans and stepped into the doorway with both hands raised.

"It's okay," John said in a low voice. "I don't have a gun. You're in charge."

"Damned right."

Lily stared, paralyzed by fear. Not for herself but for John. She wanted a future with him. She wanted forever.

"Now, Lily." Hawley's voice was a harsh bellow. "Don't play games with me. I'll kill Kirshner and your boyfriend, too."

"You don't need her," John said. "The person you're really after is Robert Prescott. Right?"

"Don't tell me what I want." There was another burst of gunfire. "Three seconds, Lily."

"I can take you to where Prescott is hiding," John said. "It's not too far from here."

Hawley ignored him. "I'm counting, Lily. One… Two…"

She didn't have a choice. She stepped through the kitchen door with her hands raised. "I'm right here."

"Come closer," he said.

"What do you want?"

"I want to pay you back for making me look bad. I'm going to make sure you never humiliate another man with your cute little karate moves."

She noticed that John had shifted his weight to his right foot. If she kept to the left, Hawley might be distracted. John might be able to get off a shot. Even if they couldn't bring him down, it was a chance. Maybe their only chance.

She sidestepped to the left. "You look good in that SWAT armor, Hawley."

"I should have been part of the team. I would have been great."

"They need guys like you," she lied. If there was one thing the police didn't need, it was a psycho in body armor. "You know the equipment. And bombs, too."

"Oh, yeah. That explosion on Cuerva was a thing of beauty. Too bad you weren't in the room. I almost got you before when I firebombed that other PPS chick's apartment."

"And the gas station," she said. "The Molotov cocktail that killed Lenny."

"That was sweet."

She edged farther left, hoping to give John a good angle. "You're really something, Hawley."

"Hold it," he said. "Before I deal with you, there's something I need to take care of."

He fired three shots point-blank into Kirshner's back. The businessman toppled face forward to the floor.

"You said you wouldn't kill him." Lily heard the tremble in her voice.

"I lied."

Another shot rang out. Hawley's arm jerked upward. Lily dove to the floor.

Two more shots. Hawley's legs crumpled. As he fell, he tried to turn. Another precision shot diverted his weapon. His gun fell to the floor.

With her weapon braced in both hands, Evangeline Prescott strode through the front door and stood over Hawley, who was on his back writhing in pain.

John picked up Hawley's gun. He flipped up the face guard on the helmet and pointed his gun at Hawley's nose. "Don't move."

In seconds, he stripped off the body armor and checked for other weapons. Fastened to Hawley's belt, he found a grenade. "I should shove this down your throat. Payback for Lenny."

"That's enough," Evangeline said. "Cuff him."

"I don't know what made you come here, but I'm glad you did," John said. "That was some nice shooting."

"It's good to know I haven't lost my touch." She

tossed her head, and her long blond hair rippled. "Are you okay, Lily?"

Still sitting on the floor, she nodded. The sudden release of tension left her in a state of shock. Too weak to stand. Struggling to catch her breath.

Evangeline frowned. "I believe my husband is somewhere nearby."

"Here." Robert stepped into the doorway from the kitchen.

Before Lily's eyes, Robert transformed. As he walked toward his wife, his nervous tension vanished. The exhaustion that weighed upon him lifted. He became the suave MI6 agent who had, several years ago, swept Evangeline off her feet. They fell into each other's arms.

With Hawley cuffed and on his belly, John came to her and held out his hand to pull her to her feet. "You did good, rookie."

"I thought we were dead."

"Looks like we have a second chance." He grinned. "This time, I'll try not to blow it."

"What do you mean?"

He continued to hold her hand. His thumb gently stroked her palm. "I love you, Lily. More than anything I've ever felt. Logically, such a love should lead to marriage. But we don't have to make those plans right away."

"I've made up my mind," she said.

He leaned back. An expression akin to fear flickered in his eyes. "And?"

She looked around the room. Robert and Evangeline were still kissing, oblivious to everything around them. Ted Hawley groaned and struggled against his cuffs while his wounds bled on the Navajo rug. Drew Kirshner lay dead. This would be one hell of a story to tell their grandchildren.

"I love you, John. Enough to marry you." She pressed her index finger into his chest. "But it's going to be a very long engagement."

"I'll wait…forever."

* * * * *

Don't miss the exciting conclusion of
BODYGUARDS UNLIMITED, DENVER,
COLORADO, *when Jessica Andersen reveals
the secrets behind the conspiracy.
Look for* CLASSIFIED BABY *next month,
only in Harlequin Intrigue.*

Every Life Has More
Than One Chapter™

Award-winning author Stevi Mittman delivers
another hysterical mystery, featuring Teddi
Bayer, an irrepressible heroine, and her to-die-
for hero, Detective Drew Scoones. After all,
life on Long Island can be murder!

*Turn the page for a sneak peek
at the warm and funny fourth book,
WHOSE NUMBER IS UP, ANYWAY?,
in the Teddi Bayer series,
by STEVI MITTMAN.
On sale August 7*

> "Before redecorating a room, I always advise
> my clients to empty it of everything but one
> chair. Then I suggest they move that chair from
> place to place, sitting in it, until the placement
> feels right. Trust your instincts when deciding
> on furniture placement. Your room should 'feel
> right.'"
>
> —TipsFromTeddi.com

Gut feelings. You know, that gnawing in the pit of
your stomach that warns you that you are about to
do the absolute stupidest thing you could do? Something that will ruin life as you know it?

I've got one now, standing at the butcher counter
in King Kullen, the grocery store in the same strip
mall as L.I. Lanes, the bowling alley cum billiard
parlor I'm in the process of redecorating for its
"Grand Opening."

I realize being in the wrong supermarket probably
doesn't sound exactly dire to you, but you aren't the

one buying your father a brisket at a store your mother will somehow know isn't Waldbaum's.

And then, June Bayer isn't your mother.

The woman behind the counter has agreed to go into the freezer to find a brisket for me, since there aren't any in the case. There are packages of pork tenderloin, piles of spare ribs and rolls of sausage, but no briskets.

Warning Number Two, right? I should be so out of here.

But no, I'm still in the same spot when she comes back out, brisketless, her face ashen. She opens her mouth as if she is going to scream, but only a gurgle comes out.

And then she pinballs out from behind the counter, knocking bottles of Peter Luger Steak Sauce to the floor on her way, now hitting the tower of cans at the end of the prepared foods aisle and sending them sprawling, now making her way down the aisle, careening from side to side as she goes.

Finally, from a distance, I hear her shout, "He's deeeeeeaaaad! Joey's deeeeeaaaad."

My first thought is *You should always trust your gut*.

My second thought is that now, somehow, my mother will know I was in King Kullen. For weeks I will have to hear "What did you expect?" as though whenever you go to King Kullen someone turns up dead. And if the detective investigating the case turns out to be Detective Drew Scoones…well, I'll never hear the end of that from her, either.

She still suspects I murdered the guy who was found dead on my doorstep last Halloween just to get Drew back into my life.

Several people head for the butcher's freezer and I position myself to block them. If there's one thing I've learned from finding people dead—and the guy on my doorstep wasn't the first one—it's that the police get very testy when you mess with their murder scenes.

"You can't go in there until the police get here," I say, stationing myself at the end of the butcher's counter and in front of the Employees Only door, acting as if I'm some sort of authority. "You'll contaminate the evidence if it turns out to be murder."

Shouts and chaos. You'd think I'd know better than to throw the word *murder* around. Cell phones are flipping open and tongues are wagging.

I amend my statement quickly. "Which, of course, it probably isn't. Murder, I mean. People die all the time, and it's not always in hospitals or their own beds, or…" I babble when I'm nervous, and the idea of someone dead on the other side of the freezer door makes me very nervous.

So does the idea of seeing Drew Scoones again. Drew and I have this on-again, off-again sort of thing…that I kind of turned off.

Who knew he'd take it so personally when he tried to get serious and I responded by saying we could talk about *us* tomorrow—and then caught a plane to my parents' condo in Boca the next day? In July. In the middle of a job.

For some crazy reason, he took that to mean that I was avoiding him and the subject of *us*.

That was three months ago. I haven't seen him since.

The manager, who identifies himself and points to his nameplate in case I don't believe him, says he has to go into *his cooler*. "Maybe Joey's not dead," he says. "Maybe he can be saved, and you're letting him die in there. Did you ever think of that?"

In fact, I hadn't. But I had thought that the murderer might try to go back in to make sure his tracks were covered, so I say that I will go in and check.

Which means that the manager and I couple up and go in together while everyone pushes against the doorway to peer in, erasing any chance of finding clean prints on that Employee Only door.

I expect to find carcasses of dead animals hanging from hooks, and maybe Joey hanging from one, too. I think it's going to be very creepy and I steel myself, only to find a rather benign series of shelves with large slabs of meat laid out carefully on them, along with boxes and boxes marked simply Chicken.

Nothing scary here, unless you count the body of a middle-aged man with graying hair sprawled faceup on the floor. His eyes are wide open and un-blinking. His shirt is stiff. His pants are stiff. His body is stiff. And his expression, you should forgive the pun—is frozen. Bill-the-manager crosses himself and stands mute while I pronounce the guy dead in a sort of *happy now?* tone.

"We should not be in here," I say, and he nods his head emphatically and helps me push people out of the doorway just in time to hear the police sirens and see the cop cars pull up outside the big store windows.

Bobbie Lyons, my partner in Teddi Bayer Interior Designs (and also my neighbor, my best friend and my private fashion police), and Mark, our carpenter (and my dogsitter, confidant, and ego booster), rush in from next door. They beat the cops by a half step and shout out my name. People point in my direction.

After all the publicity that followed the unfortunate incident during which I shot my ex-husband, Rio Gallo, and then the subsequent murder of my first client—which I solved, I might add—it seems like the whole world, or at least all of Long Island, knows who I am.

Mark asks if I'm all right. (Did I remember to mention that the man is drop-dead-gorgeous-but-a-decade-too-young-for-me-yet-too-old-for-my-daughter-thank-god?) I don't get a chance to answer him because the police are quickly closing in on the store manager and me.

"The woman—" I begin telling the police. Then

I have to pause for the manager to fill in her name, which he does: *Fran*.

I continue. "Right. Fran. Fran went into the freezer to get a brisket. A moment later she came out and screamed that Joey was dead. So I'd say she was the one who discovered the body."

"And you are…?" the cop asks me. It comes out a bit like who do I *think* I am, rather than who am I really?

"An innocent bystander," Bobbie, hair perfect, makeup just right, says, carefully placing her body between the cop and me.

"And she was just leaving," Mark adds. They each take one of my arms.

Fran comes into the inner circle surrounding the cops. In case it isn't obvious from the hairnet and bloodstained white apron with Fran embroidered on it, I explain that she was the butcher who was going for the brisket. Mark and Bobbie take that as a signal that I've done my job and they can now get me out of there. They twist around, with me in the middle, as if we're a Rockettes line, until we are facing away from the butcher counter. They've managed to propel me a few steps toward the exit when disaster—in the form of a Mazda RX7 pulling up at the loading curb—strikes.

Mark's grip on my arm tightens like a vise. "Too late," he says.

Bobbie's expletive is unprintable. "Maybe there's a back door," she suggests, but Mark is right. It's too late.

I've laid my eyes on Detective Scoones. And

while my gut is trying to warn me that my heart shouldn't go there, regions farther south are melting at just the sight of him.

"Walk," Bobbie orders me.

And I try to. Really.

Walk, I tell my feet. *Just put one foot in front of the other.*

I can do this because I know, in my heart of hearts, that if Drew Scoones was still interested in me, he'd have gotten in touch with me after I returned from Boca. And he didn't.

Since he's a detective, Drew doesn't have to wear one of those dark blue Nassau County Police uniforms. Instead, he's got on jeans, a tight-fitting T-shirt and a tweedy sports jacket. If you think that sounds good, you should see him. Chiseled features, cleft chin, brown hair that's naturally a little sandy in the front, a smile that…well, that doesn't matter. He isn't smiling now.

He walks up to me, tucks his sunglasses into his breast pocket and looks me over from head to toe.

"Well, if it isn't Miss Cut and Run," he says. "Aren't you supposed to be somewhere in Florida or something?" He looks at Mark accusingly, as if he was covering for me when he told Drew I was gone.

"Detective Scoones?" one of the uniforms says. "The stiff's in the cooler and the woman who found him is over there." He jerks his head in Fran's direction.

Drew continues to stare at me.

You know how when you were young, your mother always told you to wear clean underwear in case you were in an accident? And how, a little farther on, she told you not to go out in hair rollers because you never knew who you might see—or who might see you? And how now your best friend says she wouldn't be caught dead without makeup and suggests you shouldn't either?

Okay, today, *finally,* in my overalls and Converse sneakers, I get it.

I brush my hair out of my eyes. "Well, I'm back," I say. As if he hasn't known my exact whereabouts. The man is a detective, for heaven's sake. "Been back awhile."

Bobbie has watched the exchange and apparently decided she's given Drew all the time he deserves. "And we've got work to do, so…" she says, grabbing my arm and giving Drew a little two-fingered wave goodbye.

As I back up a foot or two, the store manager sees his chance and places himself in front of Drew, trying to get his attention. Maybe what makes Drew such a good detective is his ability to focus.

Only what he's focusing on is me.

"Phone broken? Carrier pigeon died?" he asks me, taking in Fran, the manager, the meat counter and that Employees Only door, all without taking his eyes off me.

Mark tries to break the spell. "We've got work to do there, you've got work to do here, Scoones," Mark says to him, gesturing toward next door. "So it's back to the alley for us."

Drew's lip twitches. "You working the alley now?" he says.

"If you'd like to follow me," Bill-the-manager, clearly exasperated, says to Drew—who doesn't respond. It's as if waiting for my answer is all he has to do.

So, fine. "You knew I was back," I say.

The man has known my whereabouts every hour of the day for as long as I've known him. And my mother's not the only one who won't buy that he "just happened" to answer this particular call. In fact, I'm willing to bet my children's lunch money that he's taken every call within ten miles of my home since the day I got back.

And now he's gotten lucky.

"*You* could have called *me*," I say.

"You're the one who said *tomorrow* for our talk and then flew the coop, chickie," he says. "I figured the ball was in your court."

"Detective?" the uniform says. "There's something you ought to see in here."

Drew gives me a look that amounts to *in or out?*

He could be talking about the investigation, or about our relationship.

Bobbie tries to steer me away. Mark's fists are balled. Drew waits me out, knowing I won't be able to resist what might be a murder investigation.

Finally he turns and heads for the cooler.

And, like a puppy dog, I follow.

Bobbie grabs the back of my shirt and pulls me to a halt.

"I'm just going to show him something," I say, yanking away.

"Yeah," Bobbie says, pointedly looking at the buttons on my blouse. The two at breast level have popped. "That's what I'm afraid of."

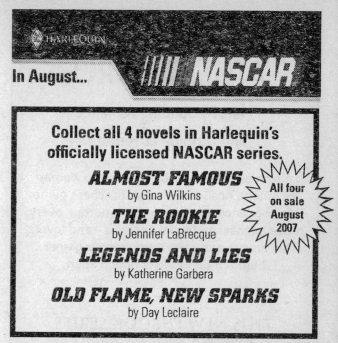

REQUEST YOUR FREE BOOKS!

2 FREE NOVELS PLUS 2 FREE GIFTS!

◆ HARLEQUIN®

INTRIGUE®

Breathtaking Romantic Suspense

YES! Please send me 2 FREE Harlequin Intrigue® novels and my 2 FREE gifts. After receiving them, if I don't wish to receive any more books, I can return the shipping statement marked "cancel." If I don't cancel, I will receive 6 brand-new novels every month and be billed just $4.24 per book in the U.S., or $4.99 per book in Canada, plus 25¢ shipping and handling per book and applicable taxes, if any*. That's a savings of close to 15% off the cover price! I understand that accepting the 2 free books and gifts places me under no obligation to buy anything. I can always return a shipment and cancel at any time. Even if I never buy another book from Harlequin, the two free books and gifts are mine to keep forever.

182 HDN EEZ7   382 HDN EEZK

Name	(PLEASE PRINT)	
Address		Apt. #
City	State/Prov.	Zip/Postal Code

Signature (if under 18, a parent or guardian must sign)

Mail to the **Harlequin Reader Service®:**
IN U.S.A.: P.O. Box 1867, Buffalo, NY 14240-1867
IN CANADA: P.O. Box 609, Fort Erie, Ontario L2A 5X3

Not valid to current Harlequin Intrigue subscribers.

Want to try two free books from another line?
Call 1-800-873-8635 or visit www.morefreebooks.com.

* Terms and prices subject to change without notice. NY residents add applicable sales tax. Canadian residents will be charged applicable provincial taxes and GST. This offer is limited to one order per household. All orders subject to approval. Credit or debit balances in a customer's account(s) may be offset by any other outstanding balance owed by or to the customer. Please allow 4 to 6 weeks for delivery.

Your Privacy: Harlequin is committed to protecting your privacy. Our Privacy Policy is available online at www.eHarlequin.com or upon request from the Reader Service. From time to time we make our lists of customers available to reputable firms who may have a product or service of interest to you. If you would prefer we not share your name and address, please check here. ☐

HI07

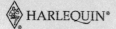

TEXAS LEGACIES: THE CARRIGANS

Get to the Heart of a Texas Family

WITH

THE RANCHER NEXT DOOR
by
Cathy Gillen Thacker

She'll Run The Ranch—And Her Life—Her Way!

On her alpaca ranch in Texas, Rebecca encounters
constant interference from Trevor McCabe, the
bossy rancher next door. Rebecca becomes very
friendly with Vince Owen, her other neighbor and
Trevor's archrival from college. Trevor's problem
is convincing Rebecca that he is on her side, and
aware of Vince's ulterior motives. But Trevor has
fallen for her in the process....

On sale July 2007

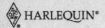

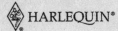